MANHUNT

Other books by this author available from New English Library:

EDGE 1: THE LONER
EDGE 2: TEN THOUSAND DOLLARS AMERICAN
EDGE 3: APACHE DEATH
EDGE 4: KILLER'S BREED
EDGE 5: BLOOD ON SILVER
EDGE 6: THE BLUE, THE GREY AND THE RED
EDGE 7: CALIFORNIA KILLING
EDGE 8: SEVEN OUT OF HELL
EDGE 9: BLOODY SUMMER
EDGE 10: VENGEANCE IS BLACK
EDGE 11: SIOUX UPRISING
EDGE 12: THE BIGGEST BOUNTY
EDGE 13: A TOWN CALLED HATE
EDGE 14: THE BIG GOLD
EDGE 15: BLOOD RUN
EDGE 16: THE FINAL SHOT
EDGE 17: VENGEANCE VALLEY
EDGE 18: TEN TOMBSTONES TO TEXAS
EDGE 19: ASHES AND DUST
EDGE 20: SULLIVAN'S LAW
EDGE 21: RHAPSODY IN RED
EDGE 22: SLAUGHTER ROAD
EDGE 23: ECHOES OF WAR
EDGE 24: THE DAY DEMOCRACY DIED
EDGE 25: VIOLENCE TRAIL
EDGE 26: SAVAGE DAWN
EDGE 27: DEATH DRIVE
EDGE 28: EVE OF EVIL
EDGE 29: THE LIVING, THE DYING AND THE DEAD
EDGE 30: WAITING FOR A TRAIN
EDGE 31: THE GUILTY ONES
EDGE 32: THE FRIGHTENED GUN
EDGE 33: THE HATED

ADAM STEELE 1: THE VIOLENT PEACE
ADAM STEELE 2: BOUNTY HUNTER
ADAM STEELE 3: HELL'S JUNCTION
ADAM STEELE 4: VALLEY OF BLOOD
ADAM STEELE 5: GUN RUN
ADAM STEELE 6: THE KILLING ART
ADAM STEELE 7: CROSS-FIRE
ADAM STEELE 8: COMANCHE CARNAGE
ADAM STEELE 9: BADGE IN THE DUST
ADAM STEELE 10: THE LOSERS
ADAM STEELE 11: LYNCH TOWN
ADAM STEELE 12: DEATH TRAIL
ADAM STEELE 13: BLOODY BORDER
ADAM STEELE 14: DELTA DUEL
ADAM STEELE 15: RIVER OF DEATH
ADAM STEELE 16: NIGHTMARE AT NOON
ADAM STEELE 17: SATAN'S DAUGHTERS
ADAM STEELE 18: THE HARD WAY
ADAM STEELE 19: THE TARNISHED STAR
ADAM STEELE 20: WANTED FOR MURDER
ADAM STEELE 21: WAGONS EAST
ADAM STEELE 22: THE BIG GAME
ADAM STEELE 23: FORT DESPAIR

MANHUNT

George G. Gilman

NEW ENGLISH LIBRARY/TIMES MIRROR

For:
Jim and Olga
who were once in
this business

A New English Library Original Publication, 1980

First NEL paperback edition January 1980

NEL Books are published by
New English Library Limited from
Barnard's Inn, Holborn,
London EC1N 2JR.
Made and printed in Great Britain by
Hunt Barnard Printing Ltd.,
Aylesbury, Bucks.

45004407 6

Chapter One

A light rain was falling out of a low and dirty grey Nebraska sky when Adam Steele thought he saw a building beside the railroad track about two miles ahead. It was as he rode his black stallion over the crest of a low rise that he received the fleeting impression of a squat, dark-coloured, frame-built structure. But a moment later the breeze veered from the east to the north and strengthened: so that the rain was driven harder and became mistlike in the far distance. And, until he was almost at the foot of the gentle slope, he could not even see the rails of the Union Pacific Railroad track.

Had the weather been fine and he firmly convinced the building existed, Steele would probably have crossed the track and continued on his south-westerly course: not interrupting his slow and steady progress until afternoon had given way to evening when he would have halted to set up a night camp.

But the prospect of a roof over his head and an opportunity to dry some of the wetness out of his clothing was too tempting to resist. So he tugged gently on the right rein to turn the horse due west, following the course of the railroad.

As far as he was able to judge, the section of line that he paralleled was between Paxton and Ogallala: this bearing taken from the fact that he had crossed the North Platte shortly after he broke camp at dawn.

Not that his precise whereabouts was of any great consequence to him. For he had no particular destination in mind when he rode away from Fort Benedict on the southern fringe of the Dakotas Badlands: merely a hankering to see once again the border country of the United States and Mexico. And that boundary was long enough to allow for a very wide margin of error.

He rode easy in the saddle towards whatever new rendezvous with fate his destiny had mapped out for him. A not very tall and, at first impression, slightly built man in his late thirties. Certainly he stood only a half inch taller than five feet six, but his frame was lean rather than slight and he was a great deal stronger than he looked.

This afternoon, in the driving rain, he fitted well into his surroundings of the green and rolling hills of western Nebraska – attired as he was in a wide-brimmed, low-crowned black Stetson tilted forward over his forehead; a knee-length sheepskin coat buttoned to the throat and with the collar turned up; medium-heeled riding boots worn inside the cuffs of blue pants; and skin-tight, black buckskin gloves.

But had the weather been fine and the topcoat lashed to the bedroll behind his saddle, he would have appeared rather incongruous against the emptiness of the western landscape. For the pants, their colour darkened by the rain, were pale blue and beneath the sheepskin coat he wore a matching suit jacket. Under this, a purple vest over a white, lace-trimmed shirt. Thus, his choice of clothing was predominantly city-style. Sometimes he enhanced his dudish appearance with a black string tie. But more often he wore a grey silk kerchief around his neck, loosely knotted at the front.

There was nothing about his face which westerners might term 'citified'. Moulded on the same lean lines as his frame, it was cut with countless lines as a result of the passage of the years and the harsh experiences he had endured in the more recent past: and was stained a dark brown by exposure to the extremes of weather.

His eyes were pitch black and his mouth-line was gentle. The bone structure which formed his features was not prominent. He wore his sideburns long but kept his hair neatly trimmed: it was prematurely grey and only when stubble sprouted on his lower face could it be seen that once Adam Steele had been red-headed.

For most of his life it could be said that he was nondescriptly handsome. But with the coming of maturity, the passing of the years and the events which filled them had acted to carve the man's strength of character into his countenance. And now, it was only when he smiled that his face looked youthful, pleasantly facile and – to the unwary – indicating a deceptive lack of moral fibre.

Adam Steele seldom smiled.

Except when there was a good-looking woman around who was smiling at him.

On this occasion the woman was a petite blonde with blue eyes and an evenly tanned, unblemished complexion. Dressed in a high-necked, tight-bodiced, straight-skirted gown with sleeves that reached to her wrists: modest in what it concealed and yet alluring in the way it contoured her upper body.

'Welcome, stranger,' she greeted from the open doorway of the building. 'I'm Lydia Karlsen. Heard you comin' in from the east. I ain't gonna need this, I guess?'

She brought her right hand around from her back to show him she was holding an Army Colt with the hammer cocked.

'Adam Steele, ma'am,' he answered, touching a gloved hand to the brim of his hat as he reined the stallion to a halt. 'You expecting trouble from the east?'

His Virginian accent was as pronounced in his voice as the day after he left the state where he was born and raised.

She shrugged her slender shoulders and gave a slight toss of her head which swung the long, ripe wheat colour hair back and forth. 'Trains come from the east and the west. Real fast and they never stop. Any man rides in from the west is from Ogallala and I'd know him. Any other direction . . .' She shrugged again. 'I got a coffee pot on the stove and the fire that's heatin' it'll dry you off some.'

'Grateful to you.'

'Barn out back where your horse'll be in from the weather. I'll be puttin' some more logs on the stove.'

Lydia Karlsen had abandoned the smile during the exchange. Now it showed, as bright and friendly as before, just as she closed the door.

Steele swung down from the saddle and, while he led the stallion around to the barn, he looked more closely at the house.

It was single storey, timber built, and from its design it suggested that it had originally been constructed as the centre section of a railroad station. For, a long time ago, there had been two doorways at the front – facing the track across a gap of some twenty feet – one of them double width. And three large windows like those usually seen in the façades of stores and office buildings. But later – still many years ago – the double doorway and one of the windows had been boarded up: and the other two windows had been reduced to the more conventional house size. The unmatched timber with which this had been done would never weather to the same extent as that used in the original construction.

The front of the building was higher than the back, to allow for the steeply pitched roof. And, just discernible here and there on the timber above the doors and windows were three widely spaced letters. Soon, they would fade away like all the others which in total had once named the building and probably proclaimed the reason for its existence.

The side and rear of the latterday house were blank of doors or windows. Out back was a sea of mud, caused by the rainwater which cascaded off the bottom of the roof's one-way pitch. Steele sank more than ankle deep into the soft ground as he led the stallion across to the barn. This was just four walls, a flat roof and a doorway. Draughts cut in through cracks in the walls, but the roof was sound. The place contained an ample supply of straw bedding, a stack of hay bales and a trough half filled with sweet water. The air smelled of fairly fresh horse droppings and from the way the place was laid out, Steele guessed just one animal was stabled here frequently. Maybe every night?

He unsaddled the stallion, gave him a brisk rub down with handfuls of dry straw and tethered him by the reins to a post so that he was out of reach of the feed and water. For these equine needs had already been taken care of during the day.

Then, leaving all his gear save for the rifle in the stable, he went out into the rain again and around to the front of the house. He used the stock of the gun to knock on the door.

'Come on in, Mr Steele,' the woman called. Then, when he pushed open the door and stepped across the threshold, she added: 'We already introduced ourselves, so there ain't no need to stand on ceremony, is there?'

As so often happened with a man like Steele – used to accepting with equanimity whatever brand of discomfort the weather threw at him – he was not aware of just how cold it was outside until he experienced the stove-heated atmosphere of the inside of Lydia Karlsen's house.

'Really do appreciate your hospitality, ma'am,' he said, taking off his hat and shaking the raindrops outside before he closed the door.

'Sure don't look like you do,' she replied without rancour from where she sat in a rocking chair to one side of a large range.

'Ma'am?' he asked as he made a quick survey of his new surroundings.

The room was a large combined kitchen and parlour with the furnishings jumbled up so that there was no clearly defined dividing line between the two functions. The range, with a rocking chair to either side of it, was against the back wall, almost opposite the door where Steele stood. There was another door in the wall to the left, in front of which was a pine table with four straight-backed chairs pushed under it. The wall to the right also had a door in it, a piano to one side of it and a needlework table littered with threads and pieces of fabric to the other. There were half a dozen closets around the walls, one of them with a large basin and water pitcher on top. There were a number of rush mats on the timber-boarded floor and several framed railroad company colour prints hung on the walls. Two unlit kerosene lamps hung from hooks in the sloping ceiling.

Thus, the comforts were minimum and Steele received an impression of Lydia Karlsen as a woman who was doing everything possible to maintain certain standards despite poverty. A situation with which he was very familiar.

'All I'm holdin' now is a cup of coffee. You've brought your rifle into my house.'

'Nothing personal,' he told her. 'Except to me. Where I go, it goes.'

'Get that wet coat off and come over here by the fire.' She rocked forward, set down her cup in the stone hearth before the stove and poured coffee from the pot into another cup.

'It your livin'?' The coffee pouring done, she got to her feet and looked at Steele as he shrugged out of the coat. 'You sure don't look the part.'

'What part, ma'am?'

'Call me Lydia.' She took his hat and coat and gestured for him to sit in the spare rocker. Then she got one of the chairs from under the dining table, set it down in front of the range and draped the sheepskin and Stetson over it. Almost immediately the dampness began to give off steam. 'Man that makes a livin' by the gun.'

The daylight which entered through the only window of the room continued to be subdued by rain and cloud. But the fire in the range grate glowed brightly and Steele was able to see the woman clearly in its flattering light.

She was about his own age. An inch or so shorter, perhaps. Weighing little more than a hundred pounds. No woman got close to forty without time taking its toll on her skin, but her wrinkles were confined to the outer corners of her eyes and to either side of her lips. Her throat above the high neckline of the dress gave a promise of the firm smoothness of her body. She wore no cosmetics and if she used perfume it was not strong enough to be detected through the aroma of strong coffee.

She was certainly good to look at: the only sour notes struck by her tone of voice and her smile. For she spoke in a monotone and her smile, which kept coming and going depending upon whether she was speaking or listening, had a forced quality about it. Almost as if she were a restaurant waitress, not happy with her job but required to show warmth to the customers – rather than a private individual who had offered, unasked, shelter and refreshment to a passing stranger.

Steele set the rifle down on the floor beside his rocker and picked up the cup of coffee.

'More like a travellin' man. Or somebody in one of the professions. Way you're dressed and all.'

The coffee was hot and strong and warming. As he took the first few sips, he saw the woman crane her neck to study the rifle.

'You don't see many like it around, ma'am,' he told her.

'Pretty old. Dates from the late fifties. Called mostly a Colt Hartford sporting rifle. I used it just the once for sporting purposes.'

She leaned back in her chair. 'I ain't much interested in guns, Adam. Didn't you say that was you name? Adam? Way I read it, it's Ben the gun was give to.'

The right side of the rifle's fire-scarred rosewood stock was uppermost and it was the inscribed gold plate screwed to the timber which had captured the woman's attention.

'It says,' the Virginian supplied, 'to Benjamin P. Steele, with gratitude, Abraham Lincoln. Ben Steele was my father. I inherited the rifle from him. Ten years ago more or less.'

'I don't mean to pry.'

'Don't consider that you are, ma'am.'

'Lydia. Just that livin' alone out here, I don't get to see many folks. Except when I go to town for supplies. Do plenty of talkin' then. Know the folks, so know what to talk about. We got nothin' much to talk on if we don't find out somethin' about each other.'

'You live here alone?'

'That surprise you?'

'Seemed to me the stable gets used. Only my horse there now.'

'My geldin's sick. Vet ain't sure what's wrong with him. So he's got him in town so he can keep a close watch on the animal.'

'You live out here from choice?' Steele asked, uncomfortably aware of the warm dampness around his legs as his pants began to steam. 'Reckon it's a long time since the trains stopped here.'

She grimaced, shook her head and then smiled sadly: and there was nothing forced about this expression. 'Trains never did stop here at Platte Creek, Adam. Except for them right at the start that hauled in the lumber to build the depot. One of the money men figured to get a town established here. But what with Paxton back down the line and Ogallala up ahead, he realised there was no call for it. So Platte Creek never did have more than the one building in it – and that not properly finished. And the trains just rattle by to them other places.'

She refilled her own cup from the pot, then leaned forward to top up Steele's.

'Seemed like a heaven-sent opportunity to Sven and me when

we come west,' she went on, and started to rock the chair gently. 'Sven got work in the sawmill over to Ogallala but there weren't no place there we could afford to live. But we got this place for next to nothin'. On account of it's twelve miles out of town.'

'Sven your husband, ma'am?'

'Lydia. Yeah, he was.' If the loss of the man caused her pain still, she concealed it well. 'Be a year on the third of next month.'

'He didn't leave you enough to move away from here . . . Lydia?'

She showed another effortless, warmer smile after he had spoken her given name. Then she nodded. 'There was enough, Adam. But after I got over the shock of what happened to Sven, I decided I liked livin' out here. See, I stayed in town for a couple of weeks . . . after it happened. Then every day started to seem like a whole month. So I came back to Platte Creek and it was much better. Guess I'm one of those kind of people that prefer their own company. For most of the time.'

Her blue eyes looked pointedly at him over the rim of her cup as she sipped at the coffee. Steele was able to recognise in the expression a tacit message that the woman considered they were kindred spirits in this respect. But her final comment caused him to look deeper into her eyes: and although he saw nothing else, he found it impossible to quell the beginnings of desire which stirred in the pit of his stomach.

He looked away from her smiling face as she lowered the cup. And had to clear a croak from his throat before he could say evenly: 'One of those that enjoy the same surroundings all the time, too.'

In the brief conversational lull while Steele searched for a broader meaning in Lydia Karlsen's expressive silence, the rain beat harder against the roof and the level of light from the window fell.

'You'll stay for supper, Adam,' she announced starkly, as she rocked the chair forward and set down her unfinished coffee in the hearth. Then got to her feet. 'No sense in gettin' all dry only to go out into this weather again. Unless you got a pressin' appointment some place else, of course?'

She stood two feet in front of him, her body and face lit from below and to the side by the glow of the range fire. By accident or design – an even stronger physical response demanded that he set his mind on reading a sexual meaning into everything she said or did – the pose and its illumination presented a tableau of erotic invitation.

Then, while the Virginian cleared a new dryness from his throat, the softly smiling woman added: 'And if you ain't already got tired of the scenery around here. You bein' the kind, I guess, that likes to be alone in lots of different places?'

'Appreciate the offer, Lydia,' Steele said. 'Happy to accept.'

She nodded and was immediately guileless again. 'Fricassee of chicken sound good? With stuffed potatoes and wild onions? Sure it does. While I get it ready, why don't you go get out of them wet pants? Sven's a few sizes larger than you. But I reckon if you wanted to get right down to the buff, one of his topcoats'd make a fine robe. And if you want, while we're eatin' supper I could put some water on to boil and you could take a bath.'

As she spoke she moved to a closet and began to take out cooking utensils and the ingredients she needed to prepare the meal.

'That door over there is the bedroom where you'll find Sven's clothes,' she went on, nodding towards the one between the piano and the work table. 'But you suit yourself, now. I ain't never been the kind of woman that tells a man what he oughta do.'

She began to hum gaily, clattering the pots and pans and ignoring Steele.

With his back to her, the Virginian finished the coffee and reached a decision. Without turning to look at her, he set down his empty cup, rose and moved across the room to the bedroom door. The woman interrupted her cheerful music making to call after him:

'Ain't no window in there, Adam. You'll find a lamp and some matches on the bureau just inside to the right.'

In the bedroom, he lit the lamp, closed the door and turned the wick low. The room was twenty by fifteen, spartanly furnished with a double bed, with a chair at the head on either side, a bureau with four drawers and a clothes closet. There were no pictures on the walls or rugs on the floor. If Lydia

Karlsen wore a nightdress for sleeping, it was not kept on the bed or under the linen.

Steele stripped off all his clothing. The first item he removed was the kerchief, which was in fact more than just that. It was a large square of silk with weights sewn into the fabric at two diagonally opposite corners which made it an effective weapon of strangulation. Steele had taken it from the corpse of an Oriental killer shortly after the end of the War Between the States. To become totally naked, he last of all unfastened the knife in a sheath which he wore strapped to the outside on his right shin and calf. He had adopted such a secretly carried weapon during the war and ever since his pants were always slit down the outside seam of the right leg: so that he could delve a hand inside to draw the knife.

While he undressed, placing each item neatly on one of the chairs, Lydia Karlsen continued to hum and to make kitchen sounds in the other room.

For a few moments – as he stood naked beside the bed and then after he had slid under the sheet and several blankets which covered it – the damply cold air and linen served to subdue the power of his urge to possess the woman. But soon, his body heat built up again and a mental image of Lydia Karlsen's stance in the firelight's soft glow sparked a resurgence of lust so intense that it was almost painful to contain.

But he resisted the impulse to call out to her. Instead lay quietly on his back, hands interlocked behind his head, gazing up at the rough hewn boarding of the roof and listening to the rain beat against the outside. For some fifteen minutes he remained so, as the woman continued to prepare the meal. For perhaps the last two minutes of this period there were no sounds from the other room. Then her knuckles rapped softly on the door.

'Adam?'

'Yes?

'Is everythin' all right?'

'No.'

'Oh?'

'There's a door between us, Lydia.'

She lifted the latch and pushed it slowly open. The lamps in the main room were now lit and were at her back. This brightness shone in her blonde hair and showed her slender figure in stark silhouette. The softer glow of the turned-down lamp in the bedroom cast the shadows of her features upwards.

Already the just-beginning-to-cook chicken flesh was giving off an appetising aroma from the pot on the range. Steele thought he had never felt less hungry in his life. Nor a greater need for a woman.

'Oh,' she said again. Softly.

'You don't have any obligation. It's just that I thought – '

'No,' she interrupted and stepped across the threshold, closing the door behind her. 'I hoped . . . but I didn't want to seem like some wanton . . . It's been a long time since the last time when Sven . . . '

He showed her the boyish smile that took several years off his true age. 'There's a limit,' he said.

She nodded. 'Yes.'

'And I think I've reached it.'

She started towards the bed, reaching up with both hands to begin unfastening the buttons of her gown at the neckline. 'I'm glad.'

'Sure hope you will be. It's not going to get any longer.'

Chapter Two

Without the moulding constraints of the gown, Lydia Karlsen's body was not as firm as it had appeared to be at first. But beneath the dress she had worn only the minimum of simple underwear. So Steele did not feel in the least cheated as he watched her shyly undress and then experienced the feel of her burning but trembling flesh against his when she came into the big bed with him.

Her body was clean and white, except at the crests of her breasts and at the hirsute areas beneath her armpits and at the base of her belly. Her nipples were enlarged and he felt the wetness of her on his thigh as she squeezed his leg between her own. Her eyes were tight closed and the touch of her fingers on his flesh was tentative.

No words were spoken. Each knew the other was ready. The woman had earlier made it known that she was not the kind to make demands of a man. And now she showed she meant what she had said, at least in the context of this most intimate of human relationships. But the part she played was expertly subservient rather than abjectly servile. So that, as Steele steered her over on to her back, eased her thighs apart and rolled on to and into her, she created cooperative counter moves: designed to heighten her own pleasure as well as stimulating his arousal. Thus was their coupling like a carefully rehearsed erotic dance, with the woman skilfully following every lead she was given – even when the man departed from the familiar routine to introduce innovation.

Still there were no words spoken. But sounds were vented

from their throats now, rasped out with increased passion between clenched teeth and compressed lips as they strove for release and yet struggled to hold back from the most delicious moment of all.

The sweat of exertion and indulgence in lust squeezed from their pores and the salt moisture mingled between their moving flesh. Steele pressed his open mouth to her tightly closed lips. She opened them and their tongues stretched for the depths of each others throats. His clawed hands became more vice-like in their hooked grip over her shoulders. She interlocked her legs more powerfully around his back. Both snapped open their eyes and saw at close range the desperate need the other felt to reach the climax of the act.

Then it came.

The woman wrenched her head to the side, tearing her lips from beneath his. And shrieked: 'Now! Please! Now!'

Steele spurted to a finish inside her and her whole being shuddered in ecstacy beneath him. She moaned and he sighed. Her legs fell away to the sides and he eased up from her, to sever the now spent connection that had joined them so pleasurably.

'Was I – ' she began, her head still screwed to the side: as if she was too afraid or too shy to look at him.

'I'm no expert, Lydia,' he replied, rolling off her and stretching out on to his back to relish the warmth and exhilarating weariness of spent passion. 'But I reckon you have no reason not to want to look at me. Unless you think it should never have happened.'

Now he turned his head on the pillow. And she rolled her head from one side to the other. So that their gazes met across a distance of less than a foot.

'Thanks, Adam.'

'Really was my pleasure,' he replied with a smile.

Her expression remained pensive. 'I didn't mean for that. Although it's made me real happy that it happened. I mean for bein' the kind of man you are. For understandin' my need and not takin' advantage of it like the kind of selfish oafs so many men are.'

She leaned her face closer to his and kissed him gently on the side of the mouth – just a mere brushing of their lips together.

Then she pulled back, sat up, swung her legs out of the bed and reached for her clothes.

'Now to see about supper,' she announced brightly as she stood up, and Steele received a final glimpse of her nude body before the dress descended to encase it. The underwear was still on the floor where she had dropped it. At the door, as she pulled it open to allow a wedge of brighter light into the room, she looked back over her slim shoulders at Steele and smiled happily. 'And afterwards, I guess it'll be too late for you to leave tonight, Adam?'

He pursed his lips and nodded. 'Reckon so. Especially if I have seconds.'

Then she closed the door behind her and began to sing: softly so that he could hear her voice and catch the melody of the song but not the words.

For more than ten minutes he lay in the comfort and warmth of the soft bed, relishing a brand of well-being that he had not experienced for a very long time. Maybe the last occasion he had enjoyed such peace of mind was before the war when, as the privileged son of one of Virginia's wealthiest plantation owners, he took such a condition for granted.

During the war, in which he rode as a cavalry lieutenant for the Confederacy, there had doubtless been some good times: periods of serene calm between the bloody battles and the brutal skirmishes when he had felt some degree of euphoria at the mere fact of his continued survival. But this evening, as he listened to Lydia Karlsen singing against the beat of rain on the roof of her Nebraska home, he chose not to cast his mind so far back into the past.

For a while he reflected, instead, upon three other women who had given themselves to him. Rosabella Sierra in Santa Fe many years ago. Renita, the Mexican whore in San Francisco. And, more recently, Marion Greenhill in Oakdale. There had been others, like Prudence Bancroft in New Orleans, Sara Yancy up in Oregon and Gemma Sellers at Fort Benedict whom he could have taken or had tried and failed.

As he examined the image of each of them in his mind's eye he was able to think kindly of just two of them. Rosabella whose offer he accepted and Gemma whom he refused. Just these two

– and now Lydia – had been prepared to share the secrets of their bodies with him for no other reason than to please him.

The rest had wanted, and in most cases had got, something in return: something beyond the simple fulfilment of desire.

But he could not blame them for this, for it was in his own nature in certain circumstances to get what he wanted at any cost.

It had certainly cost him dear to track down and kill the murderers of his father at the beginning of the violent peace which followed the ending of the war. The trail had started in a Washington bar-room where he found Ben Steele hanging from a roof beam. And ended in . . . Tennessee!

He vented a low grunt of surprise. Previously when he had reflected on the distant past he always thought of Texas as the scene of that slaughter. But no, it was definitely in Tennessee: at the fort of Colonel Fuller west of the town of Foothills, that he gunned down the men who lynched his father. And where he murdered Deputy Jim Bishop – his oldest friend – to keep from being arrested and put on trial for extracting such a terrible vengeance.

Steele grunted again and this time a grimace deepened the ruts in his weathered facial skin. In Tennessee he had killed another man who did not deserve to die. Harry Binns, in mistake for his brother Edward.

The Virginian shook his head, threw back the covers and got out of the bed: began to dress quickly. Peace of mind was not a good condition to possess if it presaged such a period of crystal clear recollection of the distant past. Better that the mental processes be disturbed by doubts about the present. In much the same way as when, after killing Bish, Steele indulged in an almost month long drinking jag in the cantina of a Mexican village.

He had not touched hard liquor or even beer since he left the Nuevo Rio cantina and yet it was as if, until today, the alcohol had continued to blot out certain memories from his mind. For what reason? Why had Tennessee been replaced by Texas in his memory? Why did he constantly recall the killing of Bish and yet have a mental block about the death of the hapless Harry Binns?

Fully dressed and uncomfortably conscious of the cold dampness of his pants around his lower legs, he had to make an effort to clear his mind of such futile questions. Way back then he did what he felt he had to do – to avenge the wanton killing of his father and then to preserve his own freedom. The cost had been high and he paid it willingly. Or was it so high? Before he fired the first shot in the violent peace he had lost everything he fought a war to preserve – except his life. Then, on the vengeance trail, he lost . . . peace of mind. Which, he had just discovered, was not a worthwhile possession. For a man such as he: who at the back of his mind had an untapped store of harsh memories which pre-dated the start of the violent peace.

Since Nuevo Rio, on the many trails he had ridden between the Mexican village and this Nebraska homestead? Many women. Many towns. Many graves. During a constant struggle to survive the dangerous circumstances which his ruling fate ordained should be used to test him. Or punish him?

With few interludes of peace and comfort such as he had been enjoying this evening – before he allowed the sourness of the past to mar the sweetness of the present.

He went to the bedroom door, managed to form his mouth-line into a smile, and opened it.

Lydia, who was midway between the range and the set for supper table, carrying a steaming cooking pot in both hands, curtailed her song. And, as she halted and turned her head, the smile which decorated her attractive face was abrubtly displaced by an expression of deep-seated terror.

But she was not looking at Steele. Instead, towards the front door of the house: which was flung open just as the Virginian stepped across the threshold from the bedroom.

Wind-driven raindrops were flung into the room.

The door crashed into the inner wall at the full extent of its arc.

The cooking pot slipped from the woman's grasp, bounced on the floor and spilled its scalding hot contents.

Lydia Karlsen screamed. Not in pain. Rather, a word. A man's name: 'Sven!'

She had said he used to be her husband. Had spoken of something happening to him – how it had shocked her to lose him.

But she never did say he was dead. '*Sven's a few sizes larger than you,*' she commented earlier. The present tense.

That was an understatement. For the man who stepped into the house was at least six feet six inches tall. With broad shoulders, a barrel chest and an enormous belly. He had to weigh close to two hundred and seventy five pounds: his belly all blubber but the rest of him solid flesh. There was just a crescent of hair around the back of his head, but it grew long down to below the nape of his neck: and in the form of a thick beard which reached to the centre of his chest. The skin on top of his head and on his face above the beard was stained dark brown by wind and sun. His eyes were pale blue and widely spaced. His nose had been foreshortened by an old break. He could have been any age between forty and fifty.

Hatless, he wore a dark grey shirt and pants, both soaked by rain. And heavy boots. He clutched a double-barrel shotgun in both his massive hands.

When he came to an abrupt halt, his frame almost filling the doorway, his dull eyes became fired with anger as they swung from his wife, to the Virginian and back again.

'You do me wrong again, woman!' he thundered, speaking English with a thick European accent. 'This time, both pay.'

As he spoke, he moved the shotgun and cocked both hammers. The twin muzzles raked first towards Steele: who knew there was no time for either words or actions – that retreat was his only chance of survival.

'Sven! Please!' Lydia screamed. As Steele threw himself backwards and sidewards. Into the bedroom and the cover of the dividing wall.

The gun roared, discharging one of its loads towards the Virginian. Steele heard the report, then a much louder sound. The latter created inside his own head as his temple slammed into the side edge of the bureau. He felt no pain. Was aware of the lesser impact as his shoulder and hip hit the board floor. He rolled on to his back involuntarily and was gripped by a sense of panic when he found he was unable to move a muscle. Just his eyes in their sockets. But at their fullest extent he could see only the blank wall beside the bureau to one side and the bed and opposite wall at the other.

'Sven, what are you doin' here – '

The second barrel of the shotgun blasted its deadly rain of scattering pellets. To Steele the woman's words had sounded shrilly loud. But then the pain of the blow to his head made itself felt and dulled his senses just as the impact had deadened his muscles. He screwed his eyes tight shut to try to blot out the abruptly intense bright light. But its source was behind the lids. He heard the gunshot like a sound which had travelled over a great distance. Then he ignored every impulse which his senses fed into his brain from outside: to concentrate his whole being on containing the urge to scream aloud in reaction to the agony trapped in his head.

It seemed to attack him for countless hours and when it was finally reduced in intensity sufficient for him to acknowledge that the world continued to exist outside of himself, he recognised that his long experience of surviving against high odds when he had his wits about him had triggered an automatic response when he was physically helpless.

For the house beside the railroad track was quiet, except for the beat of rain on its roof and against its walls. He had neither cried out nor moved – remained as silent and still as death. Had involuntarily played possum, well enough for Sven Karlsen to believe that his first shot had struck the target.

Or maybe . . . ?

Steele eased up into a sitting posture without moving his feet and lower legs which were visible from the other room. Then leaned cautiously forward to survey the scene beyond the doorway a piece at a time.

He grimaced at the pain which his actions triggered. But the expression sank no deeper into the lines of his face when he saw the great splash of crimson on the wall beside the range. Having seen this, it came as no great shock to him when his eyes settled on the almost headless corpse of Lydia Karlsen sprawled in the cold and congealing mess of spilled chicken and gravy. The blast of shot had ripped the flesh off her face and blown the top of her skull into a myriad fragments of blood-stained bone. The bodice of her gown had been shredded and her breasts were dotted with many blood run punctures.

Beyond where the woman lay in mutilated death, the table

with its two neat place settings was undisturbed. On the other side of this, the door to the house's third room was open. On to darkness and silence.

Steele got slowly and painfully to his feet and set his feet down lightly as he advanced into the room.

The front door was still folded to the wall and the wind continued to hurl raindrops across the threshold.

He moved in a half crouch, ready to delve a hand through the slit in his pants legs to draw the knife, as he swung his unblinking eyes from one open doorway to the other. He did not realise he had been holding his breath until he reached down and picked up the Colt Hartford from the floor beside the rocking chair. For then the stale air whistled out between his clenched teeth.

He thumbed back the hammer and lengthened his stride. He stepped over the body of the woman, a boot heel squelching on a piece of cold chicken. Had to go around the table to reach the doorway in the side wall.

Up close, enough light fell inside for him to see that the room was furnished as a nursery. There was a cot, a bath on a frame, a rocking horse, a case with some books on the shelves, a half dozen brightly coloured animal pictures on the walls and a number of rugs on the floor.

One of the rugs had been lifted, screwed up and tossed aside. Where it had been, two floor boards were prised up.

Steele moved into the room to take a closer look, going around to the far side of the hole in the floor before he went down on to his haunches: so that his shadow did not fall across the hiding place.

He saw a metal box with a hinged lid sunk into the ground under the house. It was about fifteen inches square and when he raised the lid – it opened easily and soundlessly – he saw it was perhaps ten inches deep. It was almost empty. Contained two coins which, when he raised them into the light, he saw were cents.

He rose to his feet and, no longer taking care to be quiet, went out into the main room of the house. The rain continued to maintain its barrage against the roof and the weather which had covered the sounds of Sven Karlsen's approach served the same purpose for another man. Who stepped out of the darkness and into the lighted doorway as Steele came around the table.

'Drop the rifle, mister, or you're dead!'

'Who is it, Max?'

'Is it him?'

Max took two more steps to come fully into the room. And thus allow entry to the men behind him. All three were middle-aged, dressed in black, ankle-length rain slickers and wide-brimmed black Stetsons. All armed with Winchester rifles which they held at hip level in unwavering aims at the Virginian.

'We're the law, mister!' Max augmented.

'Holy cow, is that Lydia Karlsen?' the man to Max's left rasped. The colour drained from his face and his rifle sagged. He looked as if he was going to be sick, but managed to swallow his bile.

Steele nodded to Max, placed the Colt Hartford on the table and stepped to the side. 'Rifle's special to me. Don't like to toss it around.'

'Sheriff, Sheriff!' a fourth man yelled in high excitement. 'Look what I found!'

He was in his mid-twenties. Hatless and wearing only a short topcoat which was not waterproof. He squeezed into the room between Max and the sick-looking man, carrying Karlsen's shotgun which was covered with light brown mud. He vented a gasp of shock when he saw the big crimson stain on the wall and the dead woman sprawled beneath it.

'Sure looks like Lydia was killed by a shotgun, Max,' the sick-looking man croaked.

'And we got us a suspect and what looks like the murder weapon, Mr Sanders,' the youngest of the quartet pointed out. 'Maybe Sven Karlsen never come here.'

'Things ain't always what they seem at first look, Quint,' Max said evenly, continuing to keep his level gaze fixed upon Steele. 'Before we start making guesses in the dark about what happened here, best we listen to what the stranger has to say.'

'Karlsen killed his wife and stole her money,' the Virginian answered.

Sanders, his pallor improved, made a sound of disgust. 'Lydia never had enough money worth stealin'!'

'You asked me and I told you,' Steele said to Max, and unclenched his left hand to reveal the coins in the gloved palm. 'My two cents' worth.'

Chapter Three

'Could be right, could be wrong,' Max allowed. 'For now I want you to go sit in one of them rocking chairs and not give Jay Sanders or Jim Adler cause to shoot you. Quint, you go back outside and keep your eyes peeled. Just in case Karlsen ain't been here already and plans on coming.'

As the youngest man went reluctantly out of the house, Steele moved across the room to occupy the rocker which Lydia had used earlier. Sanders and Adler moved forward and halted with the muzzles of their Winchesters six feet away from him.

'I'm Sheriff Tucker, by the way,' the quiet-spoken lawman announced as he moved towards the nursery doorway from which he had seen the Virginian emerge. 'Who are you?'

'Steele. Adam Steele.'

'Stranger hereabouts, ain't you?'

'That's right.'

Tucker went from sight into the nursery and made very little noise while he examined the metal box revealed by the displaced floorboards. Sanders and Adler stood nervous guard on Steele, droplets of water splashing around them to form pools.

Sanders was in his early fifties, thin faced and with a black moustache that drooped to either side of his mouth. He had a tic which periodically moved the leather-like skin under his right eye.

Adler was two or three years older, clean-shaven and with watering brown eyes that looked as if they were missing badly needed spectacles. He also had a runny nose, so perhaps it was simply that he was suffering a head cold. He had to keep taking a hand off the Winchester to raise it to his face and run the back of it across his leaking nostrils. He muttered a soft curse every time he did it.

Max Tucker came back into the lighted room and closed the door on the nursery. He had taken off his hat and unbuttoned the long rain slicker. The lawman was perhaps two or three years short of fifty. At six feet tall he matched the heights of the men aiming rifles at Steele. He had thinning brown hair which he oiled and combed flat across his head from front to back. Under his high forehead were small green eyes, too widely spaced. His nose was a little off-centre and his lips were longer and thinner than his face merited. In total the features suggested a man not to be trusted, which perhaps he realised and was the reason why he spoke in such an amicable manner to friends and strangers alike.

'There sure enough is a hidey-hole in there,' he told Sanders and Adler. 'Big enough to hold a whole bundle if it was filled up.'

Adler sniffed noisily as Tucker crossed the room to stand on the threshold of the bedroom and rake his eyes over it. 'Where would Lydia Karlsen get a bundle, Max?'

'The hole's there and it's opened up is what I'm saying,' Tucker answered, taking particular notice of something low down and to his right in the bedroom.

'Might have been put there by the railroad company when they figured to make somethin' of Platte Creek,' Sanders suggested.

'I ain't saying it wasn't,' Tucker allowed and went into the bedroom. 'Just saying what I saw.'

When he returned to the main room of the house he was carrying a blanket. Sanders sighed and Adler nodded his approval when the sheriff draped the blanket over the shattered corpse. After he straightened up from the stoop, he looked quizzically at Steele.

Sensing a particular point of interest to the lawman, the Virginian raised his gloved left hand and touched the tips of the fingers to a blood-crusted swelling on his temple. Then Tucker sat down in the second rocker, resting his rifle across the arms, his elbows on the stock and barrel and his chin against his clenched fists.

'Shoot, Mr Steele,' he invited.

The Virginian told him almost everything that had happened since he rode up to the house until he came out of the nursery and saw the sheriff at the front door. He did not mention the fact that Lydia Karlsen had joined him in the big bed for a while: claimed that the woman had suggested he might like to rest up until supper was ready.

'Makes sense,' Tucker said when he was through.

'We just got his word, Max,' Sanders said grouchily.

Adler sniffed. 'But we also got the word Karlsen busted out of the penitentiary, Jay,' he pointed out thickly, and shifted the Winchester into the crook of his arm. And was thus able to dig a handkerchief from a pocket inside his slicker and blow his nose.

'We got more than that, fellers,' Tucker put in while Sanders continued to aim his rifle and direct his scowl at the Virginian. 'Far as Mr Steele here is concerned, we can see he's got a bang on the head and I see blood on the bureau where he claimed it was done. He also told us what Sven Karlsen looks like. And him being a stranger hereabouts, he wouldn't know that unless he saw the big feller. You can add to that the fact that when I first saw him he was carrying a real fancy sporting rifle. And we all seen Lydia was blasted with a shotgun – and another barrel of shotgun lead was fired at the bedroom doorway. Just like he said.'

'Somethin' else, Max,' Adler said. 'A stranger wouldn't know about the hidey-hole, would he?'

Sanders snorted. 'It's all talk. We only got his word that he's a stranger around here. Maybe he's been in this neck of the woods lots of times. And we ain't seen him in Ogallala is all. He could've found out about the place where the money was kept from Lydia before he killed her. Hell, maybe he spent some time in the same gaol as Karlsen. He could've found out about the house and Lydia and the money from Sven: who's a long way short of bein' the brightest feller I ever met. As for the rifle and shotgun, ain't nothin' to say they both ain't his.'

'What about him bein' hit on the head and the blast aimed at the bedroom, Jay?' Adler asked. Obviously feeling ill with his cold and impatience with the talk.

'How the hell should I know?' the man with the drooping moustache snapped. 'Maybe Lydia gave him a shove and he fell. Maybe there was some kind of crazy chase in here. He took a shot at her, missed and had to fire again.'

Adler looked as if he was about to spit. Instead, he sneezed. And cursed. 'In between the two shots,' he growled sourly, 'Lydia Karlsen called time out so she could serve supper?'

'Shit!' Sanders snarled. 'She didn't have no gun handy. Maybe she figured to toss the cookin' pot at him.'

Steele saw that Tucker nodded in acknowledgement of each point which was made by both men. Finally, the sheriff sighed and rose to his feet.

'You got a horse around?'

'In the barn out back.'

'Jim, like for you to go out and get Mr Steele's mount ready for riding. Then bring the animal around to where ours are waiting?'

'You taking me in, Sheriff?' Steele asked.

'To hold as a material witness. I already told you what you said makes a lot of sense. But Jay put across some interesting things, too.' He broke off as Adler opened the front door to admit wind and rain. 'Hey, Jim. Tell Quint to come on in here and give me a hand with the deceased.'

'I'm with Adler, feller,' the Virginian drawled. 'Way Sanders guessed it is nonsense.'

Tucker nodded. 'But you're biased.'

'Reckon I am.'

'Then so is Jay,' Tucker allowed with a glance towards the scowling Sanders. 'On account of he runs the sawmill where Karlsen worked and has always said the Swede got a raw deal all the way down the line.'

'And so he did!' the moustached man growled.

Quint came into the house, still carrying the shotgun, which had now been cleaned of mud by the pouring rain. He was short and wiry with a round, pale face under a shock of black, curly hair. He had thick lips, large blue eyes and was starting to grow a moustache.

'You got a lariat on your horse, son,' Tucker told him. 'Go get it and fix the blanket around the deceased. And while you're at it, take that Colt Hartford rifle out and fix it to my saddle.'

'He do it, Mr Tucker?' Quint asked, narrowing his big eyes to look at Steele.

'He ain't under arrest, son,' the lawman answered grimly. 'And even if I have to arrest him, ain't no way of knowing if he's guilty or innocent until he's stood trial.'

The Virginian remained impassively seated in the rocker as the preparations to leave were made. Constantly under the threat of Jay Sanders' aimed Winchester.

He had never been to Ogallala but had heard of it. Just as he had heard of Abilene, Caldwell, Dodge City, Wichita, Newton and Ellsworth. Wide-open cattle-trading towns which had sprung up along the railroad tracks. Places to which the Texans drove their herds of longhorns to do business with buyers from the east and the west. Where, after the business was done and the profits made, money was spent. Rip-roaring, anything-goes towns which could be as wild as the boom towns which sprawled on the sites of gold or silver strikes. The kind of towns where justice was invariably rough and had to be quick because the gaols were not large enough to allow it to be any other way. Towns in which lawmen could make reputations for themselves by piling up convictions: and when the numbers were seen on the record books, the trials and how they were conducted had been forgotten.

Steele's reflections were based upon hearsay and maybe the stories had been exaggerated. Perhaps the worst of the railroad cow towns had been used as an unfair example of what all the others were like. Ogallala could be the most well run of them all, operating a fine legal system.

But the fact was, the Virginian did not trust Sheriff Max Tucker. The reason was nothing he could put his finger on and he felt faintly disconcerted by this. For it was in his nature to distrust every stranger until he or she proved the suspicion to be unwarranted. And Tucker had not put a foot wrong so far.

'All right,' the lawman announced when he returned to the house after helping Quint to carry the blanket wrapped body of Lydia Karlsen outside. 'As of now, Mr Steele, I got no reason to tie you up. But I'm insisting you ride into town with us. You make any move to run out on me, I'll consider it an admission of guilt. Which'll give me call to shoot you down. After which we'll take you in dead or trussed up like a Thanksgiving turkey. Jay, take him outside and get him mounted.'

Sanders gestured with the Winchester and Steele rose from the rocker and moved out of the house, taking his dried hat and coat off the chair and donning them as he went.

Quint and Adler were already in the saddles of their geldings, the older man looking ill and miserable and the younger watching Steele closely, his coat rucked up at the right side so he could rest a hand on his holstered Colt.

The woman's body was lashed into place behind the saddle of Tucker's gelding and the Colt Hartford and shotgun were slung from the saddlehorn.

Sanders waited until Steele was astride the black stallion before he mounted his horse. When he was in the saddle, he levelled the rifle again.

In the house, the range fire hissed as Tucker doused it. Then the sheriff turned out all three kerosene lamps before he came out, closing the door behind him.

'Let's go,' the lawman said as soon as he was mounted. 'You lead the way, Mr Steele. Just follow the tracks. Nice and easy. No rush.'

Even before the group of five men heeled their horses into movement, their faces were run with water and the rain had soaked deep into all their clothing except for the slickers. But only Jim Adler voiced his disgust with the weather, cursing to the unresponsive Jay Sanders who rode beside him. Tucker and Quint were ahead of this pair, immediately behind Steele, who rode a diagonal course between the front of the house and the railroad, then swung due west to comply with the lawman's directive.

He was prepared to be proved wrong in his estimation of Sheriff Max Tucker: but was not prepared to risk being behind bars in the event that his distrust turned out to be well-founded.

So, although he appeared to ride easy in the saddle, shoulders hunched under his coat and hat pulled low against the needles of rain which the norther hurled at him, he was in fact tense and edgy. And his eyes moved constantly in their sockets, trying to pierce the storm-lashed darkness: searching for some feature of the terrain that would offer him solid cover if he could make a break. Cover from which he would be able to switch from retreat to attack: for he had no intention of moving far without the familiar Colt Hartford in his possession.

But the rain made it impossible for a man to see more than twenty feet in any direction. And within that range of vision there was just the Union Pacific Railroad tracks, running arrow-straight across ground without any grades.

Grimacing in the privacy of the dark night, he recalled his thoughts when he had first closed with the railroad and turned the stallion toward the house. How he had wondered what new surprise his destiny was planning for him. Then how it had turned out to be a very pleasant surprise for a change. Until, as had always happened in the past, a brief period of luxurious tranquillity had been shattered by violence.

'The prisoner get to bed Mrs Karlsen, Mr Tucker?' Quint yelled.

It was the first comment anyone had made since they rode away from the house. And the youngest member of the posse had to shout to make himself heard against the wind and rain – even to the sheriff riding close beside him.

'Mr Steele ain't a prisoner, Quint!' the lawman replied at the same volume. 'He's a material witness.'

'Okay. So did he get to –'

'He didn't say,' Tucket interrupted. 'And it don't have no bearing.'

'It could do, Max!' Jim Adler corrected. 'If Karlsen went to the house! Could make it the same as last time!'

'Karlsen wouldn't get away with second degree again!' Tucker countered. 'Especially not if there was a big bundle in the hole.'

Far to the west, a train whistle howled. Long and mournful.

'Ten o'clock for Omaha is right on time,' Quint yelled.

Steele reined in his stallion and turned the horse sideways on to the four-man posse. The sheriff pushed forward his right hand to fist it around the frame of his booted Winchester. As Quint clawed his coat up to reach for the Colt in his holster.

'Karlsen was in prison for killing somebody before, feller?' the Virginian asked, fixing his gaze on the face of Tucker as all four men brought their horses to a check.

'So what?' Sanders demanded. 'He had good reason for what he done and there's lots of folks think he got a raw deal over it.'

'This ain't the time or the place or the weather to hang around talking, mister!' Tucker growled and for the first time since he ordered Steele to drop his rifle, there was harshness in his tone.

'Damn right!' Adler snapped. 'I could get pneumonia out here!'

The approaching train issued another mournful howl as it closed with a trail crossing. Nearer but not yet near enough for any other sound of its thundering progress to be heard.

'He killed a man he found with his wife?' Steele insisted.

'Yeah, that's what he done, mister!' Quint answered.

'And now he's escaped from gaol?'

'That's right!' Tucker snarled, and eased the Winchester halfway out of the boot. 'And Lydia didn't do or say anything much to keep him from going to the penitentiary. So the odds are her husband made a bee-line from there to the house and killed her just like you told it. If we can find him around here, you got nothing to worry about. So let's move it on out again, uh?'

They could hear the thud of pistons and clatter of wheels now. The rails were humming and the ground was starting to tremble with the vibration of the locomotive and its line of cars.

'Yeah, or we'll hog-tie you and lead you by a rope, mister!' Sanders warned, having to shout even louder to be sure his words sounded above the noise of the train.

Steele saw the rails glisten in the leading arc of the locomotive's headlight: grimaced as if in response to what he had heard, and made to tug on the right rein.

But instead he abruptly jerked on the left one, thudding his heels into the flanks of the black stallion.

The animal snorted a protest, but lunged into a sudden quarter turn and made to gallop between the mounts of Tucker and Quint.

These two men, and Sanders and Adler behind them, yelled and cursed.

The locomotive engineer saw the group of mounted men beside the track and opened a valve to blast a further warning with the steam whistle.

Each man in the posse dragged his hand away from rifle or revolver to give his full attention to controlling his spooked horse.

Of their own volition, the mounts of Quint and Adler veered to the left and those of Tucker and Sanders to the right. Clearing a path for Steele's stallion to go between. Which placed Quint and Adler dangerously close to the railroad, the hoofs of their horses kicking up cinders and thudding on ties.

The locomotive, headlight blazing and whistle shrieking, was less than a hundred feet away.

Steele steered his horse to his left and leaned in the same direction, stretching out one gloved hand. Aware that the slightest error of mistiming would likely cost him his life, he pushed his clawed hand an inch further to the left. Then closed the fingers into a fist. His expression was impassive and he allowed himself just a low grunt of satisfaction as he felt the solidness of the Colt Hartford frame in his hand.

He had already seen that Quint had used twine rather than rope to tie the rifle to the sheriff's saddlehorn. So there was just a slight check as the fastening snapped.

Then he was in back of where the four-man posse were still struggling to control their mounts: Quint and Adler desperately angling away from the track, while the less dangerously placed Tucker and Sanders sought to merely calm their animals which were rearing and turning beneath them.

Steele took no time to check on the positions of either the men or the train. He simply jerked on the right rein to command the stallion into another tight turn. And vented a yell as he again thudded his heels into the animal's flanks.

The horse was probably as terrified as the others by the sudden moves, the cacophony of sound and the blinding wedge of light. But he had been owned by this man a long time and he trusted him. So he complied without baulking to this new command. Even though he may have realised he was on a collision course with whatever was causing the noise and the light.

At the edge of the railroad, the Virginian demanded a jump and the stallion again responded instantly: lunging into a powerful leap that kept the hoofs clear of the treacherous cinders, the rails and the ties.

Steele glanced for a split second to his right and it was as if he was sailing at an incredibly slow speed across the face of the sun. Or even was held in suspension before the fires of hell.

Then the stallion hit the ground four footed, finely balanced to continue with the gallop which his rider had previously demanded.

Steele felt the heat of steam and the tug of violently displaced air as the locomotive thundered by at his back. Then for stretched seconds had his way ahead illuminated by the flickering light from the passenger car windows. Next, total darkness, his eyes not yet having adjusted to the abrupt change after the caboose had raced by to be swallowed by night.

He began to ease the stallion out of the gallop then, and the animal – steam rising from his coat and venting from his flared nostrils – was moving only at a walk by the time the clatter of the speeding train had faded from earshot.

'The sneaky bastard!' Quint roared. 'He got away!'

'If he didn't get spattered by the train!' Sanders countered.

'No sign that happened, Max!' Alder reported. And sneezed.

'He didn't just get away!' Tucker snarled. 'He got away with the rifle!'

'So best we keep our voices down!' Adler called at the same volume as before: which meant that the men were still widely scattered.

Then silence, except for the hiss of falling rain.

'You did fine, boy,' Steele said softly to the stallion as he stroked the coat at the animal's neck. 'But I reckon we better get more than just one jump ahead of them.'

Chapter Four

The Virginian was aware that, although he was outnumbered, on a night like this it was to his advantage. Because four riders must by necessity make more noise than one.

Of course, there was the possibility that they might split up and use a counter advantage – their knowledge of the country. But he rejected this. They were townsmen and it was likely that the terrain this far east of Ogallala was as unfamiliar to them as it was to their quarry. Also, Max Tucker was the only professional lawman among them. Sanders was a sawmill operator. Adler looked like a businessman of some sort. And Quint . . . a store clerk, or some other kind of hired hand, he guessed. Which meant that Tucker was the only one of the quartet who was being paid to put his life on the line: and that none of them was likely to be an expert tracker in open country on a moonless night with a gusty norther lashing rain at the already sodden ground.

So Steele took no evasive action beyond putting distance between himself and the railroad track where he began his escape bid: walking the stallion and listening for any sound that was not caused by wind and rain.

It was perhaps an hour later that the storm showed signs of abating and after this only minutes before the wind dropped and the rain became a drizzle. Then the cloud began to break up and bright pinpricks of starlight showed here and there. Visibility increased by degrees and after the rain had stopped completely and a half-moon dropped fuzzy light through high cloud, Steele allowed his muscles to relax and felt the tension drain out of him.

He was riding across the same kind of grassy sandhills country as he had travelled during the day and by veering from left to right or angling in the opposite direction to go through folds between the rises, he was able to avoid being skylined. He used this tactic to put about another two miles of Nebraska land between himself and the railroad – his ultimate heading always south west – and then rode up an incline and reined the horse to a halt below the crest of the rise. There he dismounted, dropped down on to his haunches and spent several minutes surveying the terrain to the north.

The hill was the highest ground in the immediate area and after his silent survey was completed the Virginian was certain the four men were not trailing him. Yet. Or if they were, he had at least a two-mile lead on them.

He remounted, rode around the crest of the hill rather than over it, and then glanced up at the sky. Perhaps a few more stars were showing, and the moon was still a blur above streaky clouds. But there seemed little chance of more rain tonight. So the deep marks made by the hoofs of the stallion would remain in the ground for the immediate future: to show the direction in which Steele had ridden to anyone who elected to come after him.

Anyone? Sheriff Max Tucker was the only man who might take the trouble. And would he bother? On account of the murder of a woman of no local importance who, he was more than halfway convinced, was killed by her husband.

No, Steele decided, the Ogallala lawman would not come after him for this reason. Damaged pride would be his motive should Tucker come looking for tell-tale hoofprints in the rain softened ground. So how high was the sheriff's reputation in his area of jurisdiction? And how much store did he set by what the local people thought of him?

The Virginian curtailed this line of thinking which called upon him to make guesses based upon so few known facts. And looked for a place to bed down for the night. He found it in a sandy hollow almost completely encircled by low brush and as he unfurled his bedroll and chewed on some jerked beef he recalled with a frown the big bed, the full-bodied woman and the hot meal which had been either experienced or promised back at the house beside the railroad.

Then, after he had unsaddled and tethered his horse and got between the damp blankets, fully dressed apart from topcoat and hat, he felt the frown cut deeper lines into his face. And his fist tightened around the frame of the Colt Hartford which shared the bedroll. He could almost taste the sourness of his thoughts.

Because of the killings he did while avenging the murder of his father, he considered that the United States east of the Mississippi was forbidden territory to him: the river a purely arbitrary line he had drawn himself and encroached across only twice.

Long ago he had bitterly resented this as he brooded over the loss of his birthright and yearned for the unattainable opportunity to re-establish the Steele plantation to its former glory. But time and reason had prevailed upon him to accept that it was futile to dwell on impossible dreams. And in this new frame of mind he adjusted to the life of a Western drifter, initially searching for a stretch of green and pleasant land as a substitute for the Virginia plantation but then learning to be content in whatever place he elected to hang his hat. But essential to this brand of contentment was the sure and certain knowledge that he was free to move on whenever and wherever he chose, within the generous confines of the western United States.

And so, as he lay under the Nebraska sky, waiting for sleep to come, he felt far from content this night. Knowing that, unless Sheriff Max Tucker captured Sven Karlsen and proved the Swede murdered Lydia Karlsen, there was an area of country west of the Mississippi – albeit a small piece – where he was not free to go.

He slept, with the gloved fingers of his left hand pressed to the congealed blood on his temple. And dreamed of the living and desirable Lydia. Then woke when a woman said:

'Mister, you asleep?'

He snapped open his eyes and a split second later, under cover of the blankets, cocked the hammer of the Colt Hartford.

'I don't mean you – ' she began and thrust her hands out in front of her, palms toward him and fingers splayed, 'no harm, mister.'

It was lighter than when he had fallen asleep. A cold, grey light: which took nothing from the moon. The false dawn. She was almost in silhouette against the green of brush and grass and the sky from which the night cloud had disappeared.

'That's good,' he said as he sat up, so that the blankets fell away from his chest and became rumpled in his lap.

She drew in a breath sharply when she saw that his right hand was fisted around the rifle.

'Nor me, you,' he added.

He could see her more clearly now. In her early twenties, she was an inch or two above five feet tall and built on slender lines: her figure displayed by tight fitting denim pants and a check shirt that hugged close to every gentle rise and indentation of her body. She had shoulder length red hair that swept down in waves and then curled under at the bottom, to either side of a pretty, blemish free face. Her eyes were pale blue, her nose finely styled and her lips full and a little pouted. Because of her sparseness of flesh, her facial bone structure was prominent.

Steele made his brief but thorough survey of her after he had glanced all around the hollow: and decided that if he had to wake up to company, he was happy to have such an attractive stranger looking down at him.

'My name's Anne. With an *e*. Hate it when folks sound that last letter, though.'

'All right, Anne. I'm Adam Steele. I don't see any other horse but my own.'

'I didn't ride here.'

He got to his feet and slid the rifle into the boot of his saddle which rested near the unfurled bedroll. 'Then you've had a long walk, Anne. Unless I'm way off where I thought I was.'

She dropped down on to her haunches and for the first time he saw the weariness in her eyes and the way her shoulders sagged as her hands hung limply between her slim thighs. 'I came from Ogallala. It was a long walk.'

He saw, also, that her clothing – including the grey Stetson which hung down her back on the neckcord – had the stiff look of fabric which had been sodden and dried.

'You picked a bad night to take a walk in the country, I reckon.'

'I got by. Anythin's better than what I left back home. Rain and wind didn't bother me. Sure wish I'd brought some food, though.'

True dawn broke. Steele said: 'You want to build a fire, Anne? I could use some breakfast, too.'

'Sure thing,' she agreed and smiled, the parting of her lips showing a fine set of white, straight teeth. Then, as she rose up off her haunches, her expression clouded. 'But I should tell you I can't pay you. I got no money. But bein' a girl, I got me.'

'I noticed you were a girl,' Steele answered, without looking up from his chore of taking the makings of breakfast from his saddlebags. 'You don't look like that kind.'

'I ain't never been. But in my circumstances, I gotta do what I have to to get by.'

'Just build the fire,' he told her.

As she began to snap dead wood from the brush, he drew the rifle out of the boot and headed up the slope to the highest point of ground surrounding the hollow. Some birds were on the wing far to the north east but apart from these, there was no other sign of life in any direction as the leading arc of the sun showed above a distant ridge. There were a thousand places where ten thousand men could be concealed, by accident or design.

Down in the bottom of the hollow, he struck a match and touched the flame to the base of the fire she had built.

'Least I can do is cook breakfast,' she offered.

'Fine,' he answered, nodding to the heap of dried beans, salt pork, coffee, and cooking and eating utensils he had taken from his saddlebags. 'Boil some water first. Out of one of the canteens. For coffee and shaving.'

While she set to work, he rolled up his bedding and checked over the stallion to see that the horse was still fit after the leap across the railroad track and the ride over sodden grassland.

'None of my business,' she said when he was satisfied with the stallion's condition and sat waiting for the water to boil, a razor in one gloved hand and a cake of soap in the other. 'But just now, were you lookin' for somebody in particular or some other stranger like me?'

'I was just looking.'

'It just has to be on your own account, mister. Nobody gives much of a damn about me, so they won't come lookin'. Even if they knew which way I came.'

'You're welcome to breakfast,' Steele told her evenly. 'I'm kind of short on sympathy.'

She shook her head and seemed momentarily to be on the point of anger. But the fire in her eyes was faint and short lived.

'You got me wrong, mister. I don't want you to feel sorry for me. I just want you to know that by helpin' me, you ain't invitin' no trouble for yourself.'

'Fine.'

She set the pork and beans to frying and, after the water was boiled, Steele took enough to shave with and the woman poured coffee grounds into the pot. They continued to be alone with their own thoughts while he scraped off a day and night of bristles without need of any kind of mirror.

They had only Steele's eating and drinking utensils between them and she did not protest when he said she should have her breakfast first. As he reduced the fire to a few embers under the coffee pot, he said:

'You took quite a chance, young lady.'

'Leavin' home?' She shook her head.

Steele shook his head. 'Coming right up to a sleeping man out here. I might have shot you. Another man might have taken what you offered and then shot you. Without wasting good food on you.'

She shrugged her shoulders and chewed on a final mouthful of beans. 'You got enough water to spare to wash the dish?'

'Just pile it on, Anne. Reckon whatever's wrong with you isn't contagious.'

She emptied the skillet on to the plate, giving him twice what she had eaten. Then finished her coffee and refilled the cup for him. 'Took me at least ten minutes to work up the courage to come down here. From up there.' She pointed toward the crest of the rise over which Steele had ridden to come down into the hollow. 'Been followin' your horse tracks for a couple of miles or so. When I saw you down here, sleeping, my first idea was to sneak up to your stuff and steal some food. But I ain't never been a thief. If I was, I wouldn't have left town with just the clothes I'm wearin'.'

'Where are you headed?' Steele asked, and washed down a mouthful of the greasy food with some strong coffee.

She shrugged. 'This way, Denver, I guess. If I'd had the money, I'd have taken the train to whatever place I could've bought a ticket. East or west on the train.'

'Are there any towns between here and Denver?'

'I don't know. Most places in this Godforsaken country are on the railroad. Don't you want any more to eat, mister?'

'It was too much.'

'You mind?' She reached across and picked up the plate he had discarded.

He waved a hand and she began to eat what he had left.

'That why you left home? Your folks never gave you enough to eat.'

For part of a second she was again in danger of losing her temper. But confined her venting of emotion to bitterness after she had chewed and swallowed some pork. 'I don't eat like a hog usually, mister. It's just that walkin' makes me hungry and I got a lot more walkin' to do. And no way of knowin' when I'll get to eat again.'

Steele nodded, finished the coffee, got to his feet and carried his gear across to where the stallion was tethered. The sun was now fully risen above the horizon and its rays warmed his back and the nape of his neck as he saddled the horse.

'You want payin' for what you give me now, mister?' Anne asked as he turned away from the animal.

She had finished breakfast and was standing up beside the dead fire, her slim legs pressed close together and her arms hanging loosely at her sides from slumped shoulders. There was an expression of resignation to hopelessness on her pretty face.

'Find a patch of sand and clean off the dirty dishes,' he told her.

She complied eagerly, but took a long time to complete the chore, on the far side of the surrounding brush. Steele had the bedroll on the stallion, with his topcoat, jacket and vest lashed to it, by the time she returned. While he packed the eating and cooking utensils away, she stood silently waiting in the same attitude as when she offered herself to him a few minutes ago. Then, as he swung up into the saddle, she gasped. Fear sounded in the exclamation. And when he looked down at her he saw the threat of tears in her blue eyes.

'I been brought up never to take anythin' unless I give somethin' in return, mister!' she said, fast and a little shrilly. 'But if all I got doesn't make no appeal to you, maybe I could cook and clean up for you? Just until we reach Denver. Or any other place along the line where there are people?'

He reached down a hand to her and withdrew his foot from the stirrup. The threat of tears were dried by the warmth of a smile of relief which brightened her eyes.

'Gee, thanks mister!' she said breathlessly as she settled into the saddle behind him and clasped her hands together across his belly.

Because of his leanness and her slenderness, they both fitted reasonably comfortably between the horn and cantle. But the slant of the cantle forced her belly hard against Steele's rump and her encircling arms caused the twin mounds of her small but firm breasts to nudge him just above the shoulder blades.

'I don't plan on going to Denver,' the Virginian told her as he set the stallion moving. 'Until we reach someplace else, you can set the fires and clean up the camps when we're ready to leave. I'll cook when it's necessary.'

'Pa did most of the cookin' at home.'

'He was a wise man,' Steele answered wryly.

She spat to the side and rasped. 'He was a bastard!'

'If I tossed you off this horse right now, reckon you'd think the same of me.'

He felt her become tense at the words he spoke and the tone in which they were spoken. 'I don't understand, mister.'

'You ought to. We speak the same language. Don't use any more of the bad kind.'

'Oh. Sorry.'

They rode up out of the hollow and along the crest of a hill that ran south west for the best part of a mile. Despite the fact that the stallion was big and strong and the combined weights of both riders was not much heavier than some men, the Virginian demanded only a slow and easy walk from his mount. Gradually, as the heat of the sun grew and Steele maintained his habitual surveillance of the terrain he was able to check his sexual awareness of the woman who by necessity had to press her body so close to his own. And to accept her as merely another person riding the horse in back of him.

'You in trouble, mister?' she asked after a silence which had lasted more than five minutes. 'Like I said earlier, it ain't none of my business. But the way you keep lookin' around for somethin'. Or somebody. I don't know how I can, but if I can help . . . '

She gave another of her shrugs. He could not see the gesture, but he felt the movement of her breasts against his back.

'Your sheriff maybe thinks I killed a woman,' Steele answered. And immediately regretted the revelation. But he had needed to say something to divert his mind from a fresh feeling of arousal: something that would invite her to continue the talk.

'My sheriff?' she countered with more than a trace of shock in her voice.

'Max Tucker. The lawman at Ogallala. You said that's where you come from.'

'That's right,' she answered morosely after a short pause. 'More than just from that crumby town, mister. I'm anxious to get away from the sheriff, too.'

Steele reined the horse to a halt and turned his head to look into her weary face across a distance of six inches. 'Why?'

Anxiety filled her eyes and she shook her head. 'I ain't broke no laws. Except for a religious one, I guess. I don't honour Max Tucker, not no way. And he's my father.'

Steele pursed his lips and, as he turned to face front again, allowed his breath to come out as a sigh.

'I been honest with you, mister,' Anne Tucker said in a rush. 'I didn't have to tell you what I did. You ain't gonna dump me for tellin' you the truth, are you?'

It was obvious that, just like he did a few seconds earlier, the woman was regretting the words she had blurted out.

'No,' the Virginian assured her as he set the stallion moving again. 'Always play the cards I'm dealt. Two of a kind is better than nothing.'

'Two of a kind . . . ? Oh, yeah. Both of us bein' on the run from Pa. We'll beat the bas . . . beat him. And ain't it said that behind every successful man, there's a woman?'

She tightened her grasp around his waist. And rested her chin on his left shoulder so that strands of her hair brushed his ear.

'Reckon that's what they say,' Steele replied, a little huskily. 'And right now I can't fail to feel it.'

Chapter Five

'Did you kill anyone, Adam?' Anne Tucker asked after a long pause following her actions of relaxing her hold on him and easing away from his back. There was just a slight trace of nervousness in her voice.

'No – ' he began to answer, but broke off. As he reined the stallion to another abrupt halt.

'What's the matter?' the woman asked. Then saw for herself and added: 'Oh!'

They had reached the southern end of the grassy ridge and were at the head of a long, shallow valley which cut a crescent shape through the hills, swinging gently to the south east. A broad and clearly defined trail could be seen, entering the valley at the far end and following it for threequarters of its length before it angled up the western slope and went from sight over a ridge. It took the form of a three hundred feet wide strip of dried, churned up earth cutting between expanses of grass. A section of the Western Trail which stretched from San Antonio in the south as far as Miles City and Fort Bulford in the north, by way of Dodge, Ogallala, Cheyenne and Laramie. One of the many routes along which the Texan herds were driven to the railroad and the northern settlements of Montana Territory and the Dakotas.

But it was not the trail which caused Steele to halt the stallion and peer intently down into the valley. Instead, a frame building situated some hundred feet off the edge of the trail, halfway up the western slope of the valley, about a quarter of a mile from where he and Anne Tucker sat the horse.

It was a two-storey house with six windows along the upper floor at the front and four below, under a steeply pitched roof. There was a porch at the front door with a signboard on top. The painted lettering of the sign could not be read over such a distance. Countless feet and hoofs had trampled a path from the trail to the house, but grass had had time to become re-established since the last visitors had left.

'It looks like a hotel, Adam,' Anne said, using his given name for only the second time. And whispering, as if she feared her voice might carry to the house.

Steele tapped his heels against the flanks of the horse. 'The last building I saw looked like a railroad station,' he drawled. 'But nobody ever got off a train there.'

'Oh. You mean the Karlsen place. Adam! It wasn't Lydia who Pa thinks you . . .'

'Come to that, you don't look like a daughter of Max Tucker,' Steele put in as she left the sentence hanging in the pleasantly warm air.

'Pa got some other men and rode out to the Karlsen place. That's what gave me the chance to take off. It must have been Lydia. But Pa only went out there because he got a telegraph that the Swede broke gaol. Surely if Lydia was killed it was –'

'Sign over the door says the *Drover Inn*,' Steele interrupted, as they rode close enough for his narrowed eyes to make out the faded lettering on the board above the porch. 'Reckon business has been slow of late.'

The building was old. Perhaps almost as old as the house where Lydia Karlsen had died. And ravaged by weather, to a greater extent than the owner was prepared to make good. There was still glass in all the windows and the roof had been adequately patched. But the timber walls were warped and buckled from lack of preservative and the door and window frames were either bare or ugly with bubbled and peeling paint.

When he halted the stallion some twenty feet away from the front door, Steele had just one hand on the reins. The other rested on his thigh, only inches from the jutting stock of the Colt Hartford.

'So that's it,' Anne said, her voice still low. 'It looks creepy. Even in the daylight.'

She tightened her grip and pressed herself close to him again, like a young child seeking reassurance from an adult.

There was dust on the insides of the windows and on the boarding of the porch.

'You know about this place?' Steele asked her evenly, not sensing any watching eyes but noting that the dust on the floor of the porch was disturbed by footprints.

'Pa never allowed me to mix with the cowpunchers that come to Ogallala. But I heard lots of stories from the other girls that were luckier. Way it's told, a hermit lives here. Grandfather of the two brothers who built and run the place years ago. The two boys got killed in a stampede and ever since then the old man ain't had nothin' to do with the cowpunchers that drive cattle by here.'

'Damn right, missy!' a man called from the other side of the paint peeled door. 'I don't allow no one inside of this place! Ain't done for eight years! Don't intend to change now! So you two better ride on by and leave us alone, you hear?'

It was the voice of an old man. High and shrill and strained. As if he was on the verge of a burst of bad temper he was making an effort to control.

'I have money if you have a horse for sale, feller,' Steele called.

From his elevated position on the rise a few minutes earlier, he had seen there was an out-building in back of the hotel, large enough to stable several horses.

'I ain't had no horse in years.'

'He don't never come to town for supplies or anythin',' Anne whispered. 'They say he lives off the wild land, like an Indian.'

'They say right, missy!' the old man yelled, proving that the passing years had done little to impair his hearing. 'I used to fight Injuns way back, before I saw it was better to learn from them. Now I don't need nothin' from no man, white or red. So you people move on out. I had enough company for one day.'

'Company?' Anne said, the word little more than a rush of air from her pouted lips.

Steele ignored her. 'How about some water, feller?' he called. 'For the horse and to refill our canteens.'

'Water enough in the hills, mister! If a man knows where to

look for it. And if he don't know where to look, he's a fool for ridin' this country!'

The man's voice was shriller in tone now, as his patience began to run out. Steele stared hard at the door which was not yet shaded from the morning sun by the porch roof. There were several cracks and knot holes in it, to which the old man might be pressing an eye. And maybe a gun muzzle. Certainly if he lived off game, he had to have a weapon of some kind. But would it be a gun? Eight years was a long time for a supply of ammunition to last.

'Need to rest the horse,' the Virginian announced as he drew both feet from the stirrups and raised a knee to bring his left leg up and over the neck of the stallion. 'And the lady and me could use some shade for awhile. We don't have to come inside for that.'

'I told you to move on out!'

Steele was already on the ground, his back to the hotel as he reached up to help the anxious-looking woman out of the saddle.

The door was wrenched open and a foot slapped down on the porch boarding.

Steele set the woman on the ground and, with his hands still on her waist, turned just his head.

The man in the doorway looked like a hermit was supposed to be. He was any age between seventy and ninety. Five feet tall and not weighing more than a hundred pounds. Dressed only in a pair of denim pants shredded at the cuffs and held up by a length of cord knotted around his waist. His feet, torso, hands, arms and what could be seen of his face were deeply ingrained with dirt. Most of his face was obscured by grey hair, hanging down from his head to several inches below his shoulders and sprouting from his cheeks and chin in an equally long beard. His skin was dark brown and crinkled and his dark eyes were deep set in their sunken sockets.

He and the interior of the house smelt of every brand of human waste. He was holding a bow with an arrow fitted to the taut string.

'I ain't had me a deer or even a jack rabbit in weeks, mister!'

the bowman snarled. 'But the way I recall it, human meat ain't too bad if a body's hungry enough.'

'Oh, my God!' Anne Tucker gasped.

'We don't mean you any trouble, old timer,' Steele said, not altering his stance. But tensed to hurl the woman to the ground and go down after her if the filthy man on the threshold telegraphed a decision to release the arrow.

But, rather than this, he felt sure he could see the man weakening by the moment: as if the strain of holding the bowstring taut was draining the final reserves of greatly diminished energy out of him.

'Strangers is always trouble! I told that to the boys, but they wouldn't listen! But they listen now and no answerin' back! So if you mean what you say, you just move on out like I told you! Shade's like water! If you don't know where to find it, you got no right to be out here! So scoot!'

'Let's go, Adam,' the woman urged. 'We can walk for awhile if you figure the horse needs – '

'Reckon we can do that,' he allowed, taking his hands off her waist and turning to pick up the reins. 'But just one thing, feller.'

'What?'

The arrow head, still aimed at Steele, was by degrees jutting further away from the old man's left fist as his right hand submitted to the pull of string and wood.

'Who came by earlier?'

'I never asked his name.'

'Which way was he going?'

'Same way as you, once you start to move. And if you don't move out real fast, missy will be goin' alone.'

He drew the bowstring back to the full extent of his strength again. Which was enough to power the arrow into a killing shot if his aim was true.

'Hurry, Adam,' the woman urged as she moved up behind him and bumped into him alongside the horse in her anxiety to get away from the angry old man.

'Steele!' A pause. Then: 'Hey, it's Annie!' Louder still: 'Annie!'

The Virginian's name was shouted from the ridge at the head

of the valley where he and Anne Tucker had halted for their first look at the Drover Inn.

The woman gasped as she recognised the voice of her father, snapping her head around to peer toward him as he shouted her name the second time.

Steele was already moving then: drawing the Colt Hartford from the boot, turning away from the horse and lunging toward the porch of the hotel.

The old man's attention had been diverted by the shouting and his sunken eyes did not return to look wildly at Steele until the Virginian was less than ten feet away from him. Then he vented an animalistic snarl as he jerked the bow back on target.

Steele could have killed him with ease. And his initial urge was to swing the muzzle of the rifle toward him, cock the hammer and squeeze the trigger: to rid the world of the crazy old man who had caused this new danger. But, Steele acknowledged, he had involved the old man, whose sole transgression was that he was eccentric.

So the Virginian raised the rifle, one-handed, above his shoulder: and hurled it like a spear toward the hirsute head.

'Adam!' Anne shrieked.

Hoofbeats thudded.

The old man instinctively ducked. And had no time to get the bow back to the aim before Steele was upon him.

'Bring the horse!' the Virginian yelled as he fisted a hand around the bow and jerked it easily out of the grasp of the abruptly terrified old man.

'Don't kill me, mister!'

'Come on, damn you!'

'I ain't got long now, anyway!'

First the old man to Steele. Then the woman to the horse. The old man again.

'Stay where you are, Annie!' This from Max Tucker, his words shouted above the rising volume of sound as horses galloped down into the valley.

Steele used his free hand on the sweat greasy forehead of the old man to shove him across the threshold. At the same time as he glanced back over his shoulder.

A few feet away, Anne was pulling hard on the reins of the stallion: her face crimson with effort and frustration as the horse advanced on the porch and then balked.

Off to the left, more distant but closing by the moment, Max Tucker led Adler, Sanders and Quint as a tighly bunched group of riders at a full gallop. Sunlight glinted on the revolvers in the hands of the lawman and the youngest of the group.

With a curse shaping his mouthline but unspoken, Steele elected to go to the woman rather than into the hotel to retrieve his rifle. And, the instant he took the reins and ordered Anne into the Drover Inn ahead of him, the stallion became obedient: responding to soft-spoken words and gentle urgings from a man he had come to trust over a long period.

Just for a moment, on the threshold of the hotel, as his hoofs rapped hollow sounds on the porch boarding, the horse made to back away. But more gentle words of reassurance encouraged the stallion to comply with what Steele required.

Glass shattered. A shot exploded, within the confines of the room. The galloping horses of the Ogallala posse were brought to a rearing, snorting, dust-raising halt at the centre of the churned up cattle trail.

'You come any closer and I'll kill you, Pa!' Anne Tucker yelled.

She was at the window to the left of the doorway, the Colt Hartford stock pressed into her left shoulder, thumb on the hammer and forefinger curled around the trigger.

The old man was still sprawled out on the floor after Steele had shoved him: spreadeagled on his back, his skinny body and limbs trembling and with tears streaming from his eyes.

As the Virginian led the stallion across the hotel bar-room and tethered the reins to the stairway banister at the end of the counter, the animal emptied his bowels. And the trail of droppings gave off a sweet smell that temporarily masked the evil stench which had an almost palpable presence in the hot air under the bar-room ceiling.

'You're making yourself an accessory to murder, girl!' Max Tucker called, not needing to shout so loudly now.

'Be happy to make it full blown murder if you're the one I

kill!' his daughter countered with every word coated in bitterness.

Steele threw down the bow as he crossed the room, reached around the woman and fisted a gloved hand on the rifle barrel.

She immediately surrendered the Colt Hartford to him. And smiled tightly when he whispered:

'You've paid in full.' Then, as he assumed the watch at the window, he asked: 'Be glad if you'd check on the old man. If he dies, your Pa will have a case against me.'

The men from Ogallala were still in their saddles, astride horses which were calm now, standing in a line facing the façade of the Drover Inn. Sanders on the left, then Tucker, next Adler and Quint was next to him. All of them had slid Winchester rifles out of the boots but only Quint was aiming at the window Anne had broken. And the pale-faced youngster with the embryo moustache rested the gun across his thighs at a word of command from the sheriff.

'Don't know if you planned it or just got lucky, Steele!' the tall man with the crafty looking face called. 'Whichever, I want you to send my daughter out of there!'

'We met up by chance, feller. And don't owe each other a thing. What she does is up to her.'

He stood immediately behind the window, in full view of the men outside: his rifle held two handed across his chest.

'I ain't making any deal, mister!' Tucker countered and in his voice and expression there were signs that his temper was held on a very short rein. 'When I got back to Ogallala and found she'd run off, I said the hell with her. Now I found her I still say the hell with her. On account of I've got my sworn duty to do. Anybody stands in the way of me doing that, they take the consequences. Anybody.'

'He's all right, Adam,' Anne called softly. 'Just old and shook up is all.'

'So if you figure to use her as a hostage, she ain't no good for it!' Tucker finished.

'Bart Sherwood's in there as well, Max,' Jim Adler said, his voice thick.

'I said *anybody*!' the lawman snarled.

Adler, his eyes puffy and his nostrils red from the head cold, grimaced in response to Tucker's put-down. Then leaned forward in his saddle to emphasise what he called to the Virginian. 'Look, Mr Steele. It's almost sure the Swede killed his wife. More time we waste persuading you to come in as a witness, more time Karlsen has to make tracks.'

The Virginian could actually see in Tucker's face the conscious effort the lawman made to bring his emotions under control while Adler was speaking.

Then: 'Jim's right, mister. I got to admit that you taking off the way you did, it don't look good. But I can understand why you did what you did. You being a stranger around here. Guess there's lots of lawmen in small towns wouldn't look further than you if they found you the way I did. On the murder scene and all. But I'm different – '

'You're a hypocritical sonofabitch!' his daughter cut in bitterly from the open doorway of the hotel.

Steele glanced across at her and saw that she had picked up the bow, found the arrow and fitted the shaft to the string.

'Let's quit yakkin' and do somethin', Max,' the thin-faced, black-moustached Jay Sanders growled. 'Shit to whether he trusts us or not. If he don't give himself up peaceable, I figure he's guilty. And when a murderer's guilty, don't matter if he's brought in dead or alive.'

'Way I see it, too, Mr Tucker,' Quint agreed excitedly.

'You wanna do somethin' more than talk big, Quint Ulane?' Anne taunted.

'Trouble!' the old-timer said shrilly. 'I knew it! Strangers always bring trouble!'

Steele swung his head around to look at Bart Sherwood as the man spoke the first word and struggled to sit up on the floor. He became aware that the smell of horse droppings had now merged with every other stench contributing to the malodorous atmosphere within the hotel. Then heard a grunt from outside the place, followed by the *twang* as Anne Tucker released the bowstring.

'Adam!' she rasped.

A rifle shot cracked.

Steele was staring out of the window by then, Sherwood's ranting words ringing in his ears. He had thrown the stock of the Colt Hartford up to his shoulder and then he froze: the sights aligned on the five-pointed star pinned to the shirt of Max Tucker.

But the lawman was already in process of dying: from the arrowhead that was deeply imbedded in his chest an inch below the badge. The Winchester had slipped from his hands after discharging a bullet toward the cloudless sky. He was still in the saddle but remained there for no more than three seconds. He tried to bring his empty hands up toward the arrow shaft, his face wearing an expression of deep shock. But died before he could make contact. His eyes remained open and his mouth closed. His chin fell forward on to his chest and he toppled sideways off his mount.

Jay Sanders jerked on his reins to turn his horse away from the falling corpse, a look of horror contorting his features.

As at the Karlsen house Sanders had been close to nausea, so now it was Adler who seemed on the point of throwing up.

Quint Ulane cursed and made to aim his Winchester at the hotel doorway.

Steele swung the Colt Hartford to the side and angled it down. Squeezed the trigger and sent a bullet into the dirt between the forehoofs of Ulane's gelding. The horse reared and its rider had to drop his Winchester to concentrate on controlling the animal and staying in the saddle.

'Trouble, trouble, nothin' but trouble!' Sherwood muttered, combing his beard with the fingers of both clawed hands.

'You'll get us all killed, you fool!' Adler snarled at the youngster.

Sanders half fell from his horse to squat down beside the inert form of Max Tucker. He stared briefly into the death glazed eyes of the lawman then raised his head to locate Anne at the hotel doorway.

'You've killed your father, girl!' he accused in a tremulous voice.

'He's had it comin' to him for years!' she countered, defiance in her voice, expression and stance. 'He was goin' to shoot down Adam, who's worth ten of him!'

'You'll hang for this, girl!' Sanders snarled, coming erect. 'You and Steele both! You mark my words!'

'Ride on away from here, Mr Sanders!' she flung back at him. 'And take your dead with you. Or it'll be all your graves I'll be markin'!'

Sanders, Adler and Ulane all shifted their gazes away from the woman in the doorway to peer at Steele who remained behind the window. The rifle was still levelled from the shoulder, raking gently back and forth to cover each man in turn.

'You go along with her, mister?' Jim Adler asked grimly.

'What do you think, feller?' the Virginian drawled.

Adler sneezed and cursed. 'That you are innocent of the murder of Lydia Karlsen. But must share in Annie Tucker's guilt for what has just happened.'

'Opinion noted,' Steele said. 'Now you men do what I intend to do about that murder charge.'

'Uh?' Quint Ulane grunted.

'Beat it.'

Chapter Six

It took the three of them less than five minutes to slump the corpse of Max Tucker over the saddle of his horse, lash him in place, collect the discarded weapons and begin to ride back the way they had come. And in another five minutes they were out of sight beyond the valley side, following the Western cattle trail which would lead them all the way back to Ogallala.

During this time, no words were spoken by the men outside or the two men and one woman inside the Drover Inn.

Steele remained at the broken window, rifle levelled from the hip. The woman, less composed than before, stayed on the threshold of the hotel. And Bart Sherwood continued to sit on the floor, combing his beard with his fingers and examining his filthy nails at the completion of each stroke.

After the riders had gone over the ridge, Steele looked toward the woman and said: 'Reckon you're starting to feel bad about it now, Anne.'

She allowed the bow to fall from her limp grasp and sighed, not shifting her dull-eyed gaze away from the spot where her father had died. 'I never killed anybody before.' Then she shrugged and turned away from the door and her mouth became briefly set in the line of a hard and evil smile. 'But if I had to kill anyone, I'm glad it was him!'

The Virginian bit back on the string of harsh words he felt impelled to hurl at her. Not every father was like his had been. And there was a good chance that, if she had not loosed the arrow, Steele would be dead.

'Where did you learn to shoot with a bow?' he asked as he moved toward Sherwood.

'I never used one before. I just let go the string. And got lucky.' She sensed his ambivalence and added hurriedly: 'He really was goin' to shoot you, you know. And he was good with a rifle. I might have missed him. Or hit him someplace he wouldn't die from.'

Steele halted in front of Bart Sherwood and the old man stopped combing his beard and looked up at the Virginian. There was hatred in his dark, deep sunken eyes.

'Somebody got killed out there, didn't they? This is a bad place, mister. People been killed here before. You hurt me, mister. But no matter how much more you hurt me, I still ain't got no horse for you to take. A little grub is all. And some water in the tub out back. What come off the roof in the rain.'

'Damn, we could have told them to leave Pa's horse!' Anne muttered.

'Stealing from the dead is only all right if they don't need what you take,' Steele told her. 'He needed a ride back to town. Mr Sherwood?'

'What you want? I told you about all I got.'

'You said you had company earlier on today?'

'That I did. And he didn't beat up on an old man like me. Headed on south again when I told him to leave me and the boys alone.'

'What did he look like?'

'Look like?' The crinkled, heavily bearded face showed perplexity.

'The man that came by?'

'Big,' Sherwood replied, craning back his head and squinting up at Steele. 'Lot bigger than you.'

'He have a beard like you?'

'No, not like me. Had a beard all right. But he weren't old enough for it to turn white. He had yellow hair, like Bart Junior.'

'Adam, you think it was –'

'Jack Junior, named for his father,' Sherwood cut in on the girl, 'now he was a redhead, like the missy over there. Fine boys, but strong willed. Stubborn as mules. Just wouldn't take no advice from their elders.'

The filthy old man continued to ramble, recalling how he had warned his grandsons against building the Drover Inn at a time when a reform platform was strong in Ogallala, lobbying for ordinances against gambling, whores and round-the-clock drinking within city limits.

Steele listened for awhile, as he untethered the stallion and led him toward the door. The woman went out into the fresh air and sunlight, an anxious frown on her face as she punished her lower lip with her top teeth. The old man was finger combing his beard again by then and, instead of merely relating events of long ago, was now talking to unseen companions. Or, perhaps, in his deranged mind he could see the ghosts of Bart and Jack.

Steele closed the door.

'Am I still allowed to ride with you, mister?' Anne Tucker asked, looking down at the patterns which her moving boot made in the dust.

He sucked in and expelled several lungfuls of sweet smelling air before he replied: 'Sure,' as he swung up into the saddle then freed a stirrup and offered her a gloved hand.

'Pa was popular in town. For the job he did. Jay Sanders won't have no trouble raising a posse to come after me. And if they find me, maybe they won't bother with you.'

She was looking up into his face now. He was impassive while she expressed earnestness.

'Up to you, Anne,' he told her. 'But you should know I reckon to find Sven Karlsen and turn him in to the nearest lawman. Which means I have to go wherever he's going. In the time it takes me to catch up with him, you could be long gone in another direction. From here or the first town we reach.'

She moved toward the stallion. 'I wouldn't like it to be from here,' she said, took the hand he extended again and went up into the saddle behind him.

They rode in silence away from the stinking, disused hotel and soon the sound of the old man's voice faded from earshot.

Steele was aware that the woman held on to him as lightly as possible and made an effort not to press her body against his back.

'If you did what you felt you had to, then you did right,' he said after several minutes had elapsed. During which time he had steered the stallion on a long diagonal course from one side of the valley bottom to the other: searching for and failing to find fresh horse tracks.

Perhaps another full minute slid into history before she responded to his reassuring words. 'I guess to his way of thinkin', Pa always did what he figured was right.'

'If there were no differences of opinion, everyone would die naturally. Barring accidents.'

By now the Virginian had decided that Sven Karlsen had kept to the cattle trail on the first stage of his ride away from the Drover Inn. And, unless the Swede's tracks were marked by more than just hoofprints, they would be virtually impossible to find among so many others. So Steele held the stallion on a course down the centre of the trail, constantly raking his eyes from left to right: seeking fresh horse droppings or dried wet, burned out tobacco ash, pieces of discarded food, food wrappings or any other human or animal debris.

'An accident is what I was,' the woman answered. 'He never let me forget that. But that might've been all right, I guess. If my Ma didn't die givin' birth to me. Or even if she had and I'd been a boy. So everythin' was wrong with me, right from the start.'

The discomfort of holding herself away from him finally got to her and Steele was again made strongly aware of her splayed thighs, belly and breasts pressing against his back. But her encircling arms remained loose around his waist.

'You kept him from doing what he planned?'

'When I was small, with no mother to take care of me. That was back east. In Boston. He was master of a whalin' boat. Give it up to look after me. And brought me out west, a town and a year at a time. Missed the sea for a lot of them years. But after he got to be a lawman he liked that almost as much. I was thirteen then. In Salina, Kansas. Old enough for him to be real mean to me because he figured I kept him out of the war. And the older I got, the meaner he was. Girl gettin' to be a woman needs to go out, have friends, pretty clothes, meet boys. But he never bought me anythin' except the kind of stuff like I'm wearin' now. One time he found me walkin' with a boy in Ellsworth, Kansas, he threw him in gaol and framed him for attempted rape. And took me home and tanned the hide off me.'

Steele reined the stallion to a halt and peered hard at the ground.

'What's the matter?' the woman asked.

'You ever see Sven Karlsen?'

'Lots of times. He had a job at Jay Sanders' sawmill. Rode by our place twice a day to and from work. Why?'

'He smoke?'

'A big pipe.'

'Fine.'

Steele moved the stallion forward again, away from the heap of tobacco ash which had obviously been knocked out of a pipe bowl.

'You listening to me, Adam?' Anne asked without rancour.

'Yes,' he answered, briefly recalling the bunch of six youngsters he had met up with in Oregon awhile back, heading east on Conestoga wagons: running away from over-strict parents. One of the girls had got to him then.

'After Ellsworth, he hardly allowed me out of the house at all. Any of the houses we lived in. Guess there was good reason in some of the towns where there was maybe just one unattached female to every fifty men. He did the buyin' of supplies and the cookin' and I was his unpaid housekeeper. Did his washin' and cleanin' and darnin' like I was some old woman no good for anythin' else.'

She paused, as if giving him an opening to comment. When he said nothing, she held her peace.

They were off the trail now, riding on the upgrade out of the valley to the south where the trail continued to follow the low ground, swinging eastwards. This was the route the big, blond, bearded man had taken, moving across the prairie grass when it and the earth beneath were still wet with heavy rain. Already, the morning sun had dried the ground and the hoofprints in it.

'You know anything about Sven Karlsen except that he smokes a pipe, Anne?' the Virginian asked as he crested the rise and rode down a slope into another shallow valley that ran due south: maybe all the way to the Kansas line.

'Sorry, Adam.'

'Nothing at all?'

'I mean about goin' on about myself and my troubles. But you got to understand. I never got to talk to many folks, except the few that used to come by the house. And Pa and me, we never exchange any words much. About Mr Karlsen?' She sighed and her breasts moved beguilingly against Steele's back again. 'He never came by the house. Nor his wife. So I just got to know about them from what other folks said. And a lot was said when he killed Billy Swan and got life for it instead of hangin'.'

Steele halted the stallion and Anne made to dismount.

'You stay,' he told her. 'I'll walk awhile. Closer to the sign on the ground and it'll rest the horse.'

'You want to hear things second hand?' she asked after he had started to lead the horse by the reins.

'Sure.'

'Well,' she said thoughtfully, and took a few moments to recollect old memories and organise them in her mind. 'They come to Ogallala real poor and the Swede had trouble findin' a job on account of he wasn't too smart. Which wouldn't have mattered if he'd known anythin' about cows. But he didn't. Anyway, Jay Sanders took a shine to him and give him a job at the sawmill. Wasn't nowhere in town they could live though. But then Sanders had the idea about the place out at Platte Creek. The old railroad station that never was. Of course, you know about that. Anyway, he fixed it so the Karlsens could live there.

'Everythin' seemed fine for all concerned. Until the rumours started. And if you've ever lived in a small town, you'll know it lives and breathes on gossip.'

'Big towns are the same,' Steele put in as the woman took time to organise her memories again. 'They're just a lot of small ones that have grown big.'

'But a person can get lost in one, I figure.'

Steele had been briefly in San Francisco, Chicago, New

Orleans and – long ago – Washington. 'Best thing to do is get lost from them,' he growled.

'What?'

'Nothing. What rumours?'

'About Mrs Karlsen. How she used to get visits while the Swede was puttin' in long days at the sawmill.' She paused, but not for long. 'Men, you know?'

'Reckon so?'

'Billy Swan, of course. He was a cattle agent in town. Got rich gettin' buyers and sellers together. And a real ladies' man. Figure I was the only woman in Ogallala he didn't try to get friendly with. On account of how he knew the way Pa thought of men who did more than tip their hats to me. And others, so the stories went. Jay Sanders himself. And Mr Adler the druggist. That oaf Quint Ulane. Why, even Pa come home ragin' one night. There was a story goin' around the saloons that he stopped off at Platte Creek. On his way back from takin' a horse thief to North Platte.

'But weren't any of them stories told in court when the Swede come up on a murder charge. What happened was he got took sick at the sawmill and Sanders sent him on home early. Way he told it in court, he went into the house and found his wife and Billy Swan in bed together. Sleepin', which was why they didn't hear him ride up. And the Swede just pulled out his gun and put a bullet in Billy Swan's forehead. Plumb centre. Don't mind tellin' you, Adam. When I heard what he did, it set my mind to thinkin'. About blowin' out Pa's brains all over the pillow.

'But then I didn't figure the satisfaction of that was worth spendin' the rest of my life in the penitentiary like the judge said the Swede was goin' to have to do.'

'Lydia didn't help him, is the way I heard it,' Steele said.

'That's right. Course, bein' his wife, she wasn't allowed to speak against him. But she could've gone on the stand and said how Billy Swan forced her and all. Told some lies, maybe. Instead, way I heard it, she just sat in the courtroom and stared at him like she hated his guts all through the trial.'

'Grateful for what you've told me,' the Virginian allowed. 'Filled in a lot of the gaps between what I've already heard.

What I really need to know are details like him smoking a pipe and not being too smart. Anything that could help me track him down.'

He glanced back at her and saw that her face was furrowed by a frown of strained thought. Knew she wanted to help him and was trying desperately hard to dredge some useful information from the back of her mind.

'Well, he's a Swede and he talks funny.'

'I heard him.'

'Oh, I didn't know that.'

'If he had made better time from the prison to the house, I could have been another Billy Swan,' Steele revealed, and looked back at her again.

'Oh,' she said, and her face was suddenly flushed. 'That's why he . . . '

'I don't know. But he surely killed her. Thought he'd killed me, too. Then he took some money and left.'

'Money? Way I heard it, Jay Sanders only paid him just enough for him and his wife to get by on. And after they sent him to gaol, Lydia didn't exactly start livin' high off the hog.'

'It was hidden under the floor in a room decorated like a nursery.'

'Oh yeah,' she said quickly, to capture the memory which Steele's comment had triggered. 'Lydia was carryin' a child when they first come to Ogallala. But she lost it a couple of months after they got here. Seems the Swede was real cut up about that. Way it was told, he already had a son, by the woman he was married to before Lydia. That boy turned out to be a really bad lot soon as he was old enough to take off on his own. And the Swede was hopin' the new baby would make up for that. But it wasn't to be. Kept the nursery like he planned it, though. Figured to make another baby, maybe. But that never happened, either. Who knows, if Lydia hadn't've lost the kid, things would be different today.'

After she had remained silent for over a minute, Steele asked:

'That all?'

'I think so, Adam. I'll keep on tryin' to remember, though. Maybe I'll recall some other things I heard.'

The Virginian was reluctant to waste the opportunity now that the woman's memory was functioning so well. 'He's heading south. Do you know of any particular reason he would go that way?'

'I don't.'

'His first wife? Do you know what happened to her?'

'She died is all. What of and when, I've got no idea.'

'What about his son? How old would he be now?'

'Not a boy anymore, that's for sure. Way I heard it, he took off when he was about fifteen. At least three years ago. Maybe more.'

Steele pursed his lips and allowed a quiet sigh to issue between them. 'You did fine, Anne,' he congratulated, and then spoke his thoughts aloud. 'A man on the run from a posse doesn't have to have any reason than that to go anywhere, I reckon. And the way he's built, he shouldn't be too hard to track. Long as we come across the same people he does.'

'Until the first town we come to, Adam,' she said, her voice soft and sad. 'Won't be *we* after that. And you'll be able to make better time on your own.'

It was obvious from her tone that she was not merely talking for the sake of it. But when he glanced over his shoulder, her expression gave little away. She merely gazed indifferently into the middle distance as her body moved with the motion of the horse. Apparently resigned to whatever fortune had in mind for her – certainly she made no tacit plea for the Virginian to play a positive role in what was to come.

'Your decision, Anne,' he told her as he faced forward again.

'What is?'

'Whether your take off on your own when we reach a town.'

'You mean it?' she asked, suddenly excited: like a small child more than half sure a promised treat will become a reality.

'You'll need a horse and gear and supplies.'

'I told you,' she answered, deflated. 'I got no money. And it'll take me time to earn some.'

'Maybe I'll stake you.'

She slid off the saddle with a yell of delight, came up beside him and took hold of his arm.

'You're a real nice guy, you know that, Adam Steele?' she

said with a tremulous sigh as she pressed her thigh against his and turned her upper body slightly toward him, so that the swell of her breast nudged his arm: as she gazed at his profile. 'Way I feel now, there ain't nothin' we couldn't do together.'

'Way you feel now,' he drawled, 'something sure springs to mind.'

Chapter Seven

Three long, hot, slow moving days and four short, restless, frustrating nights elapsed until they found Sven Karlsen's grey gelding.

The fact that Steele and Anne Tucker had just the one mount between them made little difference to the pace of their progress. For to track a lone rider across the short grass country of the eastern Great Plains was a slow and painstaking process. The weather stayed hot and dry during the day and the clear, brightly moonlit nights were cold. The Virginian spent more time walking than astride the horse, concentrating his attention on the sparse sign left by the Swede: while Anne Tucker watched – with diminishing enthusiasm – for a first sight of renewed pursuit. At each night camp, after they had eaten sparingly from their supplies, they took turns at standing watch.

They exchanged few words after their first full day and night together as they swung to the south west, moving out of Nebraska and into Colorado Territory. Certainly neither of them said nor did anything more which the other might construe as an invitation to put their relationship on a more intimate basis.

For his part, Steele was by turns irritated and relieved by the woman's attitude. By day, when he occasionally relaxed his vigil and glimpsed Anne Tucker's tightly clad body outlined against the clear sky: and at night should he chance to interrupt his survey of the empty horizon to glance at her sleeping beneath his blankets, he experienced an almost painful surge of desire for her. But he was able to quickly overcome his lust with the realisation that, should the Ogallala posse close in, he would not hesitate to abandon the woman. And if this proved necessary, the decision to desert Anne would be easier to make and less hard to live with if their relationship went no deeper.

Gradually, as the days and nights went by, the woman began to run out of patience: and as her boredom increased she became more and more sullen. Steele was aware of this only when he shot glances at her in unguarded moments: and glimpsed the accentuated pout of her lips and the dullness of her pale blue eyes. But always she recovered quickly, to spread a warm smile across her face and arrange her body into an alert posture. Whenever this happened, though, she made it subtly apparent that her forced enthusiasm was for the chore in hand which just happened to be part of the same job Steele was engaged in.

Then, in the early morning of the third day, when they had come close enough to the horse carcase to recognise it for what it was, Anne came alive with genuine excitement.

'Is it Karlsen's, Adam?' she asked as she peered down from the back of the live animal at the sprawled out dead one. 'It has to be his, doesn't it?'

Steele did not answer for several seconds, while he stooped to look more closely at the grey gelding and the ground on which the horse had died. Death had been caused by a deep knife wound across the throat. Not the best or most humane way to destroy a sick or injured horse, but perhaps the only method available to the Swede. From the sign on the ground, including the stain of dried blood, the gelding had dropped in its tracks and writhed in agony for a short time before the displaced rider was able to move in close and finish the suffering. Lameness had not been the cause. A stomach ailment or a heart disease, maybe. The animal had not been hard ridden, but it was long past its prime and if Karlsen had any choice he would not have chosen such an elderly and slightly built gelding as a suitable mount for a man his size.

Before leaving the horse, the big Swede had removed the canteens, saddlebags and bedroll.

'It was his,' Steele told the woman as he straightened up and peered out over the plain which extended for perhaps a further ten miles to the south west, before a line of low hills marked the horizon. 'Took sick and Karlsen had to end the pain.'

'How long ago?'

'Twenty-four hours at least. Hard to say how much longer. Not as much as forty-eight.'

The woman was still showing excitement. 'Then he was gettin' further and further ahead of us. But now we got a chance to close up, ain't we?'

'A man on foot doesn't leave as good a trail as if he's riding,' the Virginian replied thoughtfully, as he continued to gaze toward the distant hills, across a landscape which at this time of day was not yet blurred by heat shimmer. 'We just have to hope he keeps on going the same way as from the start.'

They rode double again, Steele asking the stallion for a fast walk. Pleased by the faster pace, Anne Tucker held tightly to Steele's waist and from the feel of her red hair against his neck he knew she was more conscientious in her survey of their back trail.

The Virginian altered his course twice during the length of the morning it took to reach the first upgrade into the hills. The first time when he spotted a canteen some two hundred feet to the left. Then, three hours later, he veered to the right to pass close by a pair of saddlebags. He did not dismount to examine the abandoned articles for it was obvious they would be empty of their former life-giving contents.

A mile into the hills, they reached a stage or supply trail. It swung from the north west toward the south east, following the line of least resistance between the high points of the low hills. Steele did not hesitate before veering the stallion to the left.

'Why this way, Adam?' the woman asked after a few minutes of silence. 'There's no way of knowin' that he even took the trail?'

'He took the trail,' the Virginian answered. 'He's out of food and even if he started out with two canteens, he's running low on water. Trails are made by men travelling between two places where there were or still are other men living. Reckoned he'd keep heading in the same general direction as he always was.'

'Karlsen might figure that to double back up north could throw the posse off.'

'By all accounts, he's not very bright. But he could think that way. He's been walking for a long time. Way I see it, he'll reckon that if the posse hasn't caught up with him yet, then the men from Ogallala have already been thrown off.'

There was another silence, lasting a full minute. Then Anne pointed out: 'We haven't exactly been scorching the prairie with our speed. Maybe we lost them.'

'Or they're biding their time.'

'Why should they do that?'

'There'll be a whole bunch of them. Four at least, maybe a lot more. Been fine days and clear nights. Would have been difficult for men to close in on us without us seeing them out in the country we just crossed.'

'You know what?'

'What?'

'I figure you have to be as smart as they say Sven Karlsen is dumb.'

'There's as much winning done by dumb luck as by being smart, Anne.'

'But you never count on it.'

'Take what comes,' he answered as he reined in the stallion and made the necessarily awkward dismount by raising and swinging a leg over the neck of the animal. Then he went round to the other side of the horse and slid the Colt Hartford out of the boot.

'What's the matter?' she asked anxiously, looking nervously in every direction.

'Behind these hills there are maybe just other hills. Maybe not.'

She made another suspicious survey of their surroundings and then nodded as Steele, the rifle canted to his left shoulder, began to lead the horse along the trail. 'I sure ask some dumb questions sometimes, don't I?'

'You've led a sheltered life is all,' he offered.

It was ten minutes later, as they went between two thirty-feet-high escarpments that they saw the man. And, a moment later, he saw them.

He was seated on the lowered tailgate of a covered wagon which was parked off the trail a quarter of a mile ahead in the shade of a stand of timber. A tall, thin man dressed city style in a grey suit, vest and derby hat. His torso and head were half turned to the right as he shaved, peering at his image in a piece of broken mirror propped against a carpetbag at the end of the tailgate. It was in the mirror that he first glimpsed the strangers.

The Virginian realised this from the way in which the man froze for part of a second: his posture suddenly rigid as the straight razor in his right hand was stilled halfway through a downward stroke on his lathered left cheek. Then the man recovered from his surprise but not his fear: continued with the shave while his anxious attention was directed elsewhere.

'Why, it's Mr Corder,' Anne Tucker said with quiet excitement. Then raised her voice to shout: 'Hello, Mr Corder!'

Steele had started to turn to look at the woman, but swung his gaze back toward Corder when she yelled the cheerful greeting. And was in time to see the startled man move his head, but not the razor. The blade cut the skin and the pure whiteness of the lather on his jaw was abruptly coloured red by escaping blood.

Corder seemed unaware of the wound as he peered toward the newcomers: obviously had not recognised the woman's voice and was not seeing her clearly yet.

Steele had continued to move at the same easy pace since seeing the man on the rear of the wagon: had simply tightened the grip of his gloved hand around the frame of the Colt Hartford and shifted his thumb to the hammer. Now, as Corder dropped the razor into a basin of water and delved a hand into the wagon at his back, the Virginian cocked the hammer and released the stallion reins – ready to bring up his right hand to receive the barrel of the rifle as it swung down from his shoulder.

But it was only a pair of wire-framed spectacles that Corder produced from behind him, to hook on the bridge of his nose and over his ears.

'It's me, Mr Corder!' the woman called, and stood up in the stirrups as if she felt this would help him overcome his short-sightedness. 'Anne Tucker! From Ogallala!'

Steele kept the rifle cocked as he regained a hold on the reins and began to lead the stallion forward again.

'Hey, Max Tucker's daughter!' the man called, and the smile which spread across his half-shaven face as he pushed himself off the wagon tailgate seemed to be more of relief than friendly warmth. 'Would you believe that!'

'You can believe it, Mr Corder!' the woman answered, then lowered her voice. 'It's all right, Adam. He's Dan Corder. A travelling man. In fabrics for dresses and suits and drapes and such like. Comes to Ogallala twice or three times a year. Always stops by the house for poker with Pa and Sanders and Mr Adler.'

Steele eased the rifle hammer forward as he veered off the trail to follow the shortest route to where the wagon was parked.

'Well I never, sure is a small world,' Corder said as Steele and the woman reached the pleasant shade of the timber. Relief was sharing his expression with curiosity, which he directed at both the Virginian and the woman.

'Adam Steele, Mr Corder. You just cut yourself.'

'I did?' He turned to raise the mirror and peer at his reflection. 'So I did. Well, there's a thing. Guess you folks turning up like that startled me. Not used to meeting up with folks on this stretch of trail. You'll pardon me if I take the time to clean myself up.'

'You go right ahead, Mr Corder,' Anne told him as she dismounted. 'Sorry we upset you the way we did.'

'Could have been worse, young lady,' the drummer said brightly as he began to shave off the remnants of his bristles, stooping low to peer into the mirror. 'I might have had the razor at my throat.'

He laughed and its sound gave the lie to his attempt at cheerfulness. It was hollow and he was obviously still very tense. Afraid, rather than merely uncomfortable, in this new situation.

'I finally got away from Pa, Mr Corder. You knew what kind of life I had there. I just walked out while he was away. Hadn't been for Mr Steele, I would've had to have gone right on back. That, or died someplace back there.'

She jerked a thumb over her shoulder as the drummer dried his face and patted at the short, shallow cut in his cheek.

His face free of lather, it could be seen that Dan Corder was in his late fifties. Well preserved, he had a lean face with a prominent bone structure, the skin stained by exposure to weather and lined by the passing of time. A lot of thick black hair showed under the brim of his hat and his tobacco-stained teeth looked to be his own. Although his build was sparse, he seemed to be strong and his movements were smooth and fluid now that he had overcome his apprehension. Only his black eyes, magnified by the thick lenses of the spectacles, had deteriorated beyond their years.

As was to be expected of a man who sold factory-made fabrics, his clothing was of good quality and well-tailored. Looking at the cleanliness and neat attire of the man, the Virginian was very conscious of his own dishevelled appearance. Shortage of water had meant that neither he nor the woman had been able to wash up since their meeting. And neither had bothered to hand-brush their clothes or even comb their hair for the past three-and-a-half days.

Anne seemed not in the least concerned by the contrast between herself, Steele and Dan Corder. Steele betrayed his thinking only by a gesture, as he ran the back of a gloved hand over the thick bristles on his jaw. It made a rasping sound.

'If you would care to, sir, you are welcome to use my humble facilities,' Corder offered.

'Like to get to town first,' Steele answered. 'Reckon there's one not far along the trail?'

'Hardly a town, sir. But you are correct, of course. The reason I halted here to make myself presentable is because I hope shortly to do some business.'

'What is it if not a town, Mr Corder?' Anne asked eagerly, as the drummer began to stow equipment back into the wagon after emptying the water from the basin.

'Fort Sherman, young lady. Just a small army post with a few dirt farms nearby. And an Indian agency.' He eyed Steele with more than a modicum of disdain, then spoke again to the woman. 'It's very foolish of people to travel this kind of country without knowing what is ahead of them.'

'I don't claim to be smart, Mr Corder!' Anne responded frostily, then clung to the arm of the Virginian. 'But Adam has good reason to be goin' – '

'Grateful if you would give Miss Tucker a ride,' Steele cut in.

Corder swallowed hard. He had obviously expected such a request, but been unable to think of an excuse to refuse. So now told the truth. 'Well, I don't know about that, sir. Anne, I consider Max Tucker a friend of mine. But I figure him to be a bad man to cross. Way things are between him and his daughter, I'd hate it to get back to him that I helped her to – '

'You don't have to worry about Pa,' the woman interrupted, her tone still cold. 'He ain't in no position to – '

'How far to Sherman?' Steele asked.

Corder pointed along the trail to where it went from sight between the fold of two rises. 'Couple of miles beyond those hills.

'Well, it don't matter then!' Anne muttered with a scornful glance at the drummer. 'After how far we come, Adam, we can make that the same way as always. We don't need him.'

Steele ignored her. 'How far back the other way to the nearest settlement, feller?'

'Twenty miles or thereabouts. Course, there's a few shacks near waterholes in between. And an abandoned army post. Like that the whole length of this trail between Cheyenne up Wyoming way and Amarillo, Texas. On account that this is an old army supply trail. Not used much these days, since most of the posts aren't manned any more. But if you want to get fresh supplies and maybe rest up for awhile with a roof over your head, best bet is Fort Sherman. Two miles beyond those hills. I'll see you there, no doubt.'

He turned to move along the side of the wagon and climb up on to the seat. The two-horse team had remained in the traces during the halt beneath the trees. As soon as Corder was out of sight, Steele gestured for the woman to climb up into the rear of the wagon. And grasped her at each side of her narrow waist to give her a boost.

'But – ' she began.

Steele shook his head and said softly: 'I don't trust him. Prefer to get to the fort ahead of him.'

'But what if he – '

'He won't,' Steele rasped, and tipped her unceremoniously over the tailgate just before Corder shifted the brake lever and cracked the reins to urge the team into movement.

The woman showed anger and fear and neither emotion was abated by the foolish smile which Steele directed at her as she was carried away and he swung up into the saddle.

'See you in awhile!' he called, and heeled the stallion into a gallop.

His words were shouted loud enough for both the woman and the drummer to hear them above the thud of hooves and creak of wagon timbers. But Corder did not realise they were directed at two people until the stallion galloped past him and he saw the Virginian was the only rider.

'Hey, where's the Tucker girl?' the man on the wagon seat roared.

'She's been having a rough ride,' Steele rasped through clenched teeth bared in a grin as he widened the gap between himself and the lumbering wagon. 'Slipped her into something more comfortable.'

Chapter Eight

The army post of Fort Sherman was not enclosed by a stockade. It was comprised of a cluster of stone and timber constructed buildings surrounded by a broad, five-feet-deep dry ditch with a plank bridge on the east side. On the other side of the trail from the bridge was a row of frame buildings which, like those of the fort, were all single storey. Whereas the barrack, stable, armoury and guardhouse of the fort were well preserved the civilian establishments were in various degrees of disrepair.

As Steele rode off the open trail and along what was probably termed a street between the row of civilian buildings and the curve of the ditch, there were few signs of life. Smoke rose from a few chimneys, a single uniformed cavalryman stood sentry duty under the arch on the fort side of the bridge, a dog lay panting in the stoop shade out front of the Sherman Indian Agency and an old man slept with his hat over his face in a rocker to one side of the Sherman Café entrance. The Stars and Stripes hung limply in the still air from the top of the mast on the roof of the army barracks.

In addition to the agency and the café, the non-military section of Fort Sherman boasted a general store and a rambling building with a sign on the roof proclaiming it the Stopover Hotel.

The sentry glanced at the newcomer, spat into the dust at his feet and returned to an examination of his fingernails.

The dog barked, howled and then resumed panting.

The old-timer spoke without raising the hat from his face

as the Virginian halted the stallion in front of the café.

'I sells grub, coffee, beer and liquor, mister. You can get a room, bath and rent Beth Lee by the hour or the night at the hotel. Store sells more or less what you'd expect a hardware store to sell. All that's if you're a stranger to Sherman. If you been here before, I been wastin' the time of both of us. Time I got plenty of.'

Steele pushed his hat on to the back of his head and ran a gloved hand over his sweat-tacky forehead. 'Stranger, feller. Grateful for the information. Any other strangers been through here recently?'

The Virginian had judged the man's age from his scrawny torso and arms which were only partially covered by a ragged undershirt. When the man removed the Stetson – old and made of shiny black leather like his pants – it revealed a darkly stained, deeply lined countenance of someone at least eighty years of age. With grey hair, moustache and eyebrows above sightless eyes – open but fixed with a glazed stare on the middle distance.

'I do the Chamber of Commerce stuff for nothin', mister. Everythin' else I do costs.'

'The whole place work on the same lines, feller?'

'I charge a dollar. You can shop around if you've a mind. But most people take pity on me, because of my affliction, I guess. I don't see.'

'So how do you find out information people need to know?'

'Mostly I just listen, mister. Every now and then I have to ask. People who do see, they hardly ever listen.'

Steele pursed his lips, nodded and swung down from the saddle. He led the stallion to the rail and hitched him there. Took a dollar from his hip pocket and pressed it into the outstretched hand of the blind man.

'Looking for a big Swede built like a Conestoga without wheels. He treads heavy and speaks English with an accent.'

The old man parted his lips to show a smile that was all gums and no teeth. 'You understand my affliction, mister. Ain't many folks that can see would have described him like that. Figure you for a real smart feller.'

'I've already been told that today and it didn't cost me a dollar.'

'Hey now, don't get grouchy, mister. Your boy was through here. About this time of the afternoon yesterday. Came in on his own two legs. No horse. From the north. Blonde hair and good lookin' as all get out, if you can believe Beth Lee. But dumb, the way I hear it. Bought a horse off Joe Maguire at the agency and paid more than double what the nag was worth. Or maybe it was just he wasn't in no position to hang around hagglin'. Left soon as he had the horse and gear and some supplies from the store. And drank a beer in my place. Didn't talk much to no one except them he had to buy the stuff he needed. Rumoured he was on the run. From you, mister?'

'No. He go south?'

'Yep. Like I said, twenty-four hours ago. On a fresh horse. Amount of time it takes you to have refreshments won't make much difference on a lead that long. Well, I'll be, this is gettin' to be quite a day. More folks comin' in, I hear.'

He cocked his head to one side as Steele glanced out along the trail. The drummer's wagon had been in sight for several minutes, but was now close enough for the sound of its approach to reach Fort Sherman.

'Dan Corder's rig,' the blind man said. 'I'll be cookin' for Dan. Like me to make enough for two, mister?'

'Three,' Steele said as the blind man rose from the rocker. 'Or better make that four. The lady eats enough for two.'

The man was obviously intrigued by Steele's knowledge of the eating habits of a woman riding with the fabric salesman. 'You mean old Dan Corder has got himself a ladyfriend, mister?'

'She's just on loan to him,' the Virginian replied as he followed the blind man into the café.

'Oh, one of that kind. Beth Lee won't be pleased to hear that.' He vented a crackling laugh. 'Boys from the fort will be happy with a change, though.'

Steele was surprised to discover that he had to make a conscious effort to bite back on a retort in defence of Anne Tucker's honour. Particularly since, not so very long ago, he had determined to leave her for the Ogallala posse if circumstances demanded it.

'Just start the food cooking, feller,' he said tightly.

The tension his tone of voice revealed was detected by the blind man, but no comment was made as the owner of the café moved skilfully among the half dozen tables and went through an open doorway at the end of the counter which ran along the rear wall.

'You mind if I wash up and shave here, feller?' Steele asked, following the old-timer through into a kitchen that achieved the same standard of cleanliness as the combined saloon and restaurant which was the only part of the establishment the public was supposed to see. The Virginian had eaten in many better places: and a lot that were worse.

'Hotel charges fifty cents for a bath, mister. Leave it up to you what you pay for what you want. I ain't greedy. Obliged if you'd put everythin' back where you found it after you're through. Man with my affliction has to know exactly where things are.'

There was a kettle of simmering water on the range and Steele poured just a little of this into a basin and replaced it with fresh from a pitcher. There was a cake of soap on the shelf beside the basin. Since the place was run by a blind man, there were no mirrors around. As Steele washed his hands and face, rinsed the trail dust from his hair and used his host's razor to scrape thick bristles off his jaw, cheeks and throat, the old-timer began to cook a meal of ham and grits and peas without ever putting a hand or foot wrong.

Steele placed another dollar bill under the cleaned-up razor and went out into the public area to hand-brush dust off his clothing.

'Twice what you'd pay for a bath along at Beth Lee's place,' the blind man called. He claimed not to be greedy, but was obviously anxious to know what kind of reward his attitude earned. 'Appreciate that. You give me a bonus, I'll give you one, mister. That big feller with the funny way of talkin'. He's headed for Mexico.'

Steele looked back through the doorway into the kitchen which was now filled with the appetising aromas of the cooking food. 'He came right out and said that?'

'Drank a beer in my place. Heard him ask one of the men from the fort how far was it to Chihuahua.'

'Grateful to you,' the Virginian acknowledged and moved across the room and out into the sunlight as the wagon of the fabric salesman came to a creaking halt in front of the hardware store which was next to the café.

'Hi there, Mr Corder!' the sentry called across the street.

'Afternoon, Dan.' This from a man inside the hardware store.

'Good to see you again, Danny.' The most enthusiastic welcome of all from a heavily built woman in her late thirties who came out of the hotel on the other side of the store, a bright smile pasted to her thickly painted face. But the smile was short lived, replaced by a scowl of resentment.

As he moved toward his horse Steele was not in a position to see the front of the wagon and assumed Beth Lee's displeasure was caused by the sight of a younger and prettier woman sitting up on the seat beside Corder. This was confirmed when Sherman's lone whore was driven to deepen her scowl as the soldier guarding the fort grinned and yelled:

'Hey, Mr Corder. That a sample of a new line you're peddlin'?'

'Cut out the cracks, trooper!' the drummer snarled. 'And start doing your job!'

The forty-some year old enlisted man with a scar on his forehead was abruptly perplexed – and ready to be angry – by what was obviously unusual behaviour by Corder.

'Adam!' Anne Tucker yelled, her voice shrill with fear. 'He's gonna – '

There was a sharp cracking sound – of a hand against flesh. And the woman screamed her pain.

'There's a man in Blind Jake's place, trooper!' Corder roared. 'He's wanted for murder up in Ogallala!'

Steele indulged himself with a terse groan as the whore and the trooper swung their surprised attention toward him. Then he took a final step to close with his horse, and slid the Colt Hartford out of the boot: had it cocked and levelled before the fort sentry could get a two handed grip on his Spencer carbine.

The scar faced man in uniform froze, with his lips in the shape of an unspoken curse.

'Move yourself, man!' Corder ranted. 'He also had a hand in killing the Ogallala sheriff!'

'Move it yourself, mister!' the trooper snarled, and only his eyes were released from the immobilising effect of his fear. 'I don't want him to have no hand in killin' me.'

'You mean . . . ?'

The drummer, his tone of authority replaced by nervousness, leaned sideways so that he could look back along the street. His mouth remained open but his voice was stilled by the shock of seeing the Virginian with the levelled rifle.

'Watch out, Danny!' the tubby whore warned.

But Corder was too slow to react – suddenly tumbled off the wagon seat. Obviously propelled by a powerful shove by Anne Tucker. He shrieked his alarm, but the woman's voice was louder as she urged the team to move, snapping the reins above their backs.

The wagon lurched forward.

Corder's shriek became a howl of pain as he thudded to the sun baked ground.

A shrivelled old man with a limp emerged from the hardware store, glanced fearfully toward Steele and then stooped painfully to mutter words of comfort at the drummer.

Corder flung up an arm to knock the man aside and peer at his departing wagon: fanned a hand in front of his face to clear the dust which the wheelrims and team hoofs had raised.

'My wagon!' he screamed. 'Get after her!'

Steele shifted his attention briefly away from the sentry beneath the arch. To rake his eyes over the score or so of officers and men who were emerging from the fort buildings in response to the disturbance. The shouted questions of the military personnel all but drowned Corder's pleas for action to retrieve his wagon.

But the Virginian was able to hear the words of Blind Jake, spoken from just beyond the threshold of his café.

'I got a geldin' out back of the place. Nothin' on him but reins and bridle. But he ain't been ridden in four days.'

There was no time to query the blind man's motives or

ponder the alternatives. The wagon was now too far out of Sherman to be of immediate concern to anyone except it's frantic owner. And in the ditch-encircled fort officers were drawing their side arms and snapping orders for men to fetch their carbines. Only the sentry, under threat from the levelled Colt Hartford, remained unmoving. Until Steele whirled and lunged for the café doorway.

Then the man brought up his carbine and thudded the stock into his shoulder as he dropped down on to one knee and took aim.

'Ogallala trouble ain't got nothin' to do with me, mister!' Blind Jake growled as Steele sprinted across the café and saloon. 'And a man with my affliction appreciates kindness.'

The sentry's carbine exploded a shot across the street and the sightless old-timer groaned, staggered and knocked over a chair before he was able to steady himself with a two-handed grip on a table edge.

Steele came to an abrupt halt on the threshold of the kitchen and looked back at the man: saw the bloodstain expand on the tattered undershirt from the exit wound of the carbine bullet which had tunnelled through Blind Jake's shoulder – in at the back and out of the front.

'Move yourself, mister!' the man rasped through his pressed-together gums, then turned and staggered out on to the street. 'You shot me, you trigger happy bastard!' he shrieked. 'Friggin' army! Ain't my affliction bad enough? You gotta shoot a hole in me?'

His shrill words and the sight of the blossoming blood stain at his right shoulder drove the Fort Sherman soldiers into silence. Steele's booted feet thudded on the kitchen floor. As he wrenched open the rear door, Blind Jake recommenced his briefly interrupted tirade against the trooper who shot him, strengthening his taunts with a stream of obscenities.

The piebald gelding was tethered in a lean-to stable to the right of the door. The horse was older and smaller than the stallion abandoned by Steele. He turned to gaze dolefully at the newcomer, then showed his teeth in a loud snicker as the Virginian reached around him to unhitch the reins from a wooden peg.

'Right now,' Steele growled as he hauled himself up astride the bare back of the piebald, 'I don't have time to look a gift horse in the mouth.'

Chapter Nine

There had always been a string of fine horses kept on the Steele Plantation before the war. And from an early age, the Virginian had been involved with breaking-in, schooling and getting the best out of the replacement mounts which were purchased from time to time. So he had developed an expert understanding of horseflesh which went beyond the mere riding of animals.

Blind Jake's piebald resented having a bareback rider and began to buck the moment Steele was astride him. Steele was lifted into mid-air, but kept a grip on the reins and managed to wrench them to the side – turning the horse's head toward the stable doorway – before he thudded back down again, and dug his heels hard into the animal's flanks.

The chance to achieve freedom to gallop across open country after four days of being tethered in the stable took precedence in the piebald's mind over the need to unseat a strange rider. And the horse lunged out into the sunlight and fresh air. Across the back lots of the café, the hardware store and the hotel.

Steele gave the animal his head for the first hundred yards, the rifle and reins gripped tightly but the reins slack: crouching against the forward-thrust neck, pressing his elbows, thighs, knees and heels hard against the quivering flesh. Only then did he tug lightly on the left rein, to angle away from the rear corner of the hotel, to take full advantage of the building's cover until he was beyond effective carbine range of the fort.

He glimpsed the hurtling wagon for a moment, just before it went from sight over a low rise a half mile south east of Sherman. Then a crackle of gunfire told him he had been spotted by the men at the fort. The hail of bullets reached beyond the horse and rider, but none had the accuracy to match its velocity.

Steele pulled on the right rein now, before he reached the foot of a rise, to veer the piebald gelding toward the trail. And glanced to the right rear as another fusillade of gunfire sounded. Less shots than before, because most of the troopers were turning to run – following the orders of their officers to saddle and mount their horses.

The Virginian could not see any civilians until he was on the trail and no buildings intervened across the direction of his backward glance. They were in a group out front of the café, crouched down around the collapsed form of Blind Jake. Close to where the docile stallion stood, unconcerned by gunfire, still hitched to the rail.

An involuntary thought injected itself into Steele's mind as he widened the gap at breakneck speed between himself and Fort Sherman. That the blind old-timer, if he was still fully conscious, would be cursing the wound which was delaying the moment at which he could examine the stallion and decide if the exchange of horses had been to his advantage.

Steele cursed and rejected such a futile line of thought as he rode the freedom-saving – maybe life-saving – gelding over the rise and saw the wagon more than a half mile ahead of him. Anne Tucker was still driving the team to the limit of their speed along the trail that ran straight as an arrow between scattered dirt farms with boundaries crudely fenced with barbed wire strung on posts.

The men and women working the fields surrounding the run-down timber and tin shacks looked with scant interest at the lumbering wagon, returned to their chores and raised their heads again when Steele galloped the gelding past. Poverty stricken people for whom the West had proved not to be golden: eking a bare existence from unproductive land and totally indifferent to the troubles of others.

The wagon splashed through a shallow stream that crossed the trail and when the Virginian's mount sent up a spray of water to either side he was much closer to his objective.

Beyond the farmsteads with their watered fields, the terrain was rugged and dusty. Semi-desert country between the mid-western plain and the first low, shallow steps up toward the Colorado Plateau of the Continental Divide.

Steele was aware that his new mount, lacking the stamina of the abandoned stallion, was tiring. But then so were the two horses hauling the heavily laden wagon.

Two hundred yards. A hundred and fifty. A hundred. With every yard the gelding covered, the gap to the wagon was narrowed. The ground was almost constantly on an up grade now, the trail curving to left and right to by-pass rocky humps and gullies of varying depths. Like the surface to either side, the trail itself was rougher, little used during recent times beyond the southern limit of the Fort Sherman farmsteads. And the wagon bucked and rocked across old, baked-hard wheel ruts.

Steele shook his head to loose sweat beads from his eyelids and looked back over his shoulder. Was in time to see a group of troopers swoop over the rise far behind. Eight or ten of them. Undoubtedly astride horses better suited for hard riding across rough country than the mount of a blind man.

When he looked to the front again, the wagon had gone from sight and a pall of dust hung across the trail, at a point where it curved over the top of a gradient. He rode into the cloud, pulling gently on the reins to urge a gradual slackening of pace. Then heard a screech of brake blocks against wheelrims, snorts of protest from horses, men shouting and a gunshot.

The dust thickened and whirled as hoofs and locked wheels skidded across the broken, arid ground.

'Sonofafriggin'bitch!' a man shrieked, the piercing shrillness of his voice sufficient to sound above the din of the slithering wagon.

The ground dipped sharply beyond the top of the grade and made a sudden turn to the left: to run along the bottom of a gully for three hundred yards before it exited into another which angled off on the other side.

Steele brought the piebald gelding to a rearing halt as the dust settled on and around him. And gazed around the stretched neck of the animal to watch the wagon come to grief.

The woman had been driving the rig too fast to make the

turn. So the two team horses had kept on a straight course, up the rapidly steepening side of the gully. And they did not veer to the left until the grade was too severe to hold all four wheels of the wagon against the ground when it was sideways-on.

Three men sat astride their horses, positioned across the trail at the point where the turn was sharpest. They had revolvers in their fists and the lower halves of their faces were covered with kerchief masks.

They heard the snort of the gelding as it became four-footed again and this drew their shocked attention away from the wagon toward the Virginian. Their guns followed the same arcing course as their eyes.

The wagon came to a halt and the traces snapped. The team raced for freedom. The wagon was immobile for just part of a second, slid a few inches down the slope, then tipped.

'Watch it!'

'Shit!'

'Sonofafriggin'bitch!'

The men's fear stricken voices were vented as the slithering of wheels and then the creak of strained timber reclaimed their attention. And they looked up the slope and saw the wagon begin to cant toward them.

On the periphery of his vision, as he saw the trio of riders thud spurred boot heels into the flanks of their horses, Steele glimpsed something break loose from the wagon – falling on to the higher area of the slope rather than into the path of the doomed rig. Something . . . or someone. Lost to view as the wagon crashed on to its side and rolled over on to its back. Two wheels and the cover supports snapping like matchwood.

Had Steele not appeared on the crest of the rise when he did, the masked men would probably have survived unharmed. But instinctively they wrenched on their reins to turn their mounts away from the rifle toting newcomer. And one of them even wasted more time in blasting a wild shot in the general direction of the Virginian.

The first man to suffer as a result of the wagon wreck was sent flying from his saddle by a heavy bolt of fabric: flung forcefully out through a long rent in the canvas cover. His horse lunged into safety as the rider screamed and then became silent as he hit the ground with a sickening thud. The other two animals snorted in fear and pain as the tumbling wagon crashed into their hind quarters. Horses and riders alike were driven to the rutted trail, limbs flailing.

And a moment later animal and human cries were abruptly curtailed as the full weight of the wagon crushed the life out of burst open flesh. The momentum of the roll caused the shattered, virtually wheelless rig to begin another turning motion. But on level ground this could not be completed. For perhaps a full second, amid the whirling dust of the accident, the wreck tilted to reveal the crushed and blood-spilling corpses of three men and two horses. Then it fell back to conceal all but the animals' inert heads and necks and the lower legs and feet of two of the human victims. A sun glinting shard of bone had penetrated through flesh and denim from one of the legs.

The riderless horse had galloped from sight and earshot. The troopers were not yet close enough for the sound of their approach to be heard. So there was a sudden silence in the gully and on its rims: a stillness that was almost palpable in the aftermath of such a violent burst of sound.

Steele, sitting rigidly astride the saddleless gelding, revealed nothing of his thoughts by his impassive expression as his coal-black eyes shifted from the wrecked wagon to rake up the slope on which it had come to grief. The thud of hooves in the distance reached his ears as his gaze found and locked on that of Anne Tucker.

She half lay on her right side, supporting herself on an elbow. There was blood on her face. Not much: seeping from a small cut below her right eye. Tears were squeezing from both eyes as, with her free hand, she kneaded the flesh of a pained thigh.

'Oh, my God, they're comin'!' she forced out hoarsely. 'Take off, Adam. Leave me. Maybe they'll be content with just me.'

The Virginian glanced back over his shoulder and saw the troopers riding at full stretch toward him. They had obviously heard the din of the wreck and the two gunshots. And could certainly see him halted on the rim of the gully.

'I think I broke somethin' in my leg, Adam,' the woman called. 'I want you to know. I didn't plan to run out on you.

But I figured they had to take you. I'd have come back to try to get you away from them.'

'What you had in mind doesn't matter,' he told her, and heeled the winded gelding down the slope. 'Stay there.'

She had tried to rise, but grimaced as the move triggered a sharper pain in her leg. But she ignored his words, tried again and succeeded in getting to her feet. She cried out and beads of sweat oozed from every pore on her face.

The Virginian knew that the gelding was close to exhaustion. And saw that the woman was also in need of a long period of rest. But her leg was not broken. Maybe a bone was cracked or a muscle had been pulled. She used up a vast amount of energy and endured intense pain to reach the bottom of the gully. But she made it. Then seemed to fold slowly to the ground, out of sight on the other side of the wreckage from where he had dismounted from the gelding. But she came erect again, one of the dead men's Frontier Colts clutched in her fist.

She used the back of a hand to brush the mixture of tears and sweat from her eyes, and looked resolutely at Steele.

'Stolen from a dead man, Adam. But he don't have any more need of it. I don't aim to go to any more prisons now that I'm free of the one Pa kept me in.'

She cocked the hammer, leaned against the overturned wagon and expressed even greater determination as she swung her gaze and the Colt toward the point where the troopers would first come into sight.

'I ain't got the guts to shoot myself. But I'll make damn sure the army have to blast me.'

Steele gazed coldly across the wrecked wagon at her blood-sweat-and-tear-stained face for a stretched second. Then pursed his lips, slapped the gelding on the rump, rasped a barely audible curse and said evenly:

'Let's get the hell out of here, Anne.'

'What?' she countered, snapping her head around.

'There has to be a better place than this,' he told her, as he turned away. 'We don't have a chance here.'

He started to run, in the wake of the team horses, the dead man's mount and Blind Jake's gelding. Along the gully and then off to the right. Not until he veered in this direction, to follow the trail on a new up grade toward the south east, did he throw a glance back over his shoulder. And saw her coming after him. Still in pain from her injured leg, she gasped or cried out with every step as she weaved from side to side. Her teeth were gritted together between curled back lips and she was running blind, eyes tightly closed. Sweat was glistening on her face again. One hand was fastened to her leg while the other held on to the gun butt as though it was a lifeline.

Steele came to a halt and waited for her. Up beyond the rim of the gully, the troopers slowed their horses: obviously fearful of becoming easy targets if they rode full tilt into view.

The Virginian had to side step as the desperate, suffering woman veered to the right. She yelled shrilly as she stumbled against him: and showed the extent of her fear and disorientation when she tried to raise and swing the gun toward him.

'It's Adam, Anne!' he growled, close to her ear. And made to pick her up. Awkwardly, because of the Colt Hartford.

She opened her mouth to scream and made a second attempt to level the gun. Above the less urgent thud of hooves, Steele could hear men's voices. He mouthed a silent curse and aimed a short but powerful punch at the hysterical woman. His gloved fist caught her on the side of the jaw and she was abruptly limp. The revolver slipped from her grasp and rattled to the ground. Before she could follow it, he dropped into a crouch and leaned forward as he encircled her waist with an arm. Her unconscious form folded over his shoulder. He snatched up the revolver and pushed it into the waistband of his pants before he straightened and launched into a staggering, ungainly run: up the defile that cut off the gully to the south.

There were rock walls to either side and the ground beneath his pumping feet felt hard as rock. The blistering heat of the sun poured directly down at him from between the rims of the walls. The defile curved to the left and the steepening ground forced him to reduce speed. Then to halt – only moments before exhaustion would have caused him to pitch to the ground. He lowered Anne Tucker gently into the angle of ground and rearing rock. And forced himself to breathe more evenly. He used a forearm to brush sweat beads out of his eyes.

Up ahead, on the steadily rising slope, the cliffs had

crumbled on either side to scatter the ground with countless boulders. Clumps of brush and an occasional tree grew from pockets of soil among the rocks. There was plenty of cover in this area, but nothing substantial enough to conceal a horse. So the animals which had raced away from the wagon wreck must have made it to higher ground: through another defile which angled off to the right.

Steele stooped to regain a hold on the slumped woman, then froze. As a man called:

'Jesus, they're dead!'

'What?'

'The wagon tipped over, lieutenant! I can see legs stickin' out from underneath.'

The words carried clearly to where Steele stood, halted in the act of reaching for the woman to drag her toward covering rocks.

'Not Steele! Take care, men! He didn't go down there until after the wreck happened!'

The Virginian abandoned his attempt to get himself and the woman into cover and lowered himself to the ground, leaning his back gratefully against the rock wall. The plan to outrun the troopers of Fort Sherman had been the only one available: ill-conceived out of the need for speed. Maybe if he had taken off in a different direction from Anne Tucker, there would have been a chance to give the men the slip. But he had not even considered going his own way: despite the fact that it was she, by talking to Corder who had triggered the trouble back at Sherman.

Listening tensely to hear more words and sounds from the gully, he looked impassively down into the dirty, sweat-and-tear-stained face of the senseless woman: and did not need to search his mind and emotions for a reason for reaching his decision. Whatever the motive, her act of killing her father had solved an earlier dilemma: whether to gun down the Ogallala sheriff himself or surrender to the unknown brand of justice that was operated in the Nebraska railroad town.

He had been in her debt. And now, as voices reached his ears again, he postponed a self-examination as to whether there had been any other factors involved. For of first priority now was his response to the new situation. To surrender to the United States Army or to make a stand against them in circumstances which were nothing short of suicidal.

'Packer, Rogers, Flint, Bates!' the lieutenant shouted. 'Cover us! Rest of you men, follow me!'

Booted feet moved fast over rock and sun-baked dirt. Steele was able to visualise the scene as the four named men stood tense guard, raking their eyes and Spencers back and forth along the gully, while the lieutenant and the other men advanced on the overturned wagon.

'Shit, what a mess!' someone growled.

'Shut up, corporal! Check for signs of life!'

'Horses are dead, sure enough.'

Silence, except for the scrape of boot-leather against ground. Until a man called:

'No sign of the woman, sir!'

'Hey, that means there are two guys under there!'

'Neither of them the one that beat it through Blind Jake's place!'

'Corder didn't say nothin' about there bein' –'

'Shut up!' the lieutenant snapped. 'There's something odd about this. Sergeant, take two men and fetch some horses! We need to raise this wagon off the dead!'

Steele felt he had rested enough so that he could raise and carry Anne Tucker into cover. But such protection would be of use only if he chose to make a fight of it. For even a cursory search of the rock-scattered area by mounted men would be successful. So he remained where he was, ready to throw in his hand if the uniformed men came around the curve in the defile: unwilling to start a gunfight with so many troopers who were simply doing their duty.

He heard a number of horses being led down into the gully and brief exchanges of orders and acknowledgements as ropes were tied. Then eager yells of encouragement for the animals to take the strain. The creak of stressed timber as the wagon was tilted. Curses and exclamations of shock and horror as the blood-stained scene of carnage beneath the wreckage was revealed.

Then the wagon thudded down on to its wheelless axles.

There was a short, pregnant silence, broken when a trooper said coldly:

'Ain't no female here, lieutenant.'

'I can see that, sergeant.'

'Somethin' else plain to see, sir. Them men got their faces covered.'

'Hey, you think it's – '

'No doubt about that, Flint,' the officer interrupted, with a note of excitement in his voice. 'This is George Burke. So the others are sure to be Jimmy and Bob. It appears we finally have the Burke brothers.'

'And the Arapaho gotta get their guns and whiskey from someplace else,' the corporal responded in the same tone.

'George and his brothers must have figured this rig for an army wagon, sir,' a man said.

'What they thought doesn't matter, trooper,' the officer answered. 'All that does matter is that we've got them the best way there is. Wrap the bodies in blankets, sergeant. And load them on to horses.'

'What about Steele and the Tucker woman, sir?'

The Virginian's expression had not altered in the slightest degree while he listened to events back at the gully. Now, in the silence as the cavalry lieutenant considered the question, he merely pursed his lips and tightened his grip around the frame and barrel of the Colt Hartford.

'We did our best to help the civil authorities from a town that's a long way out of our jurisdiction,' the officer announced. 'The fugitives are long gone from here now. Load up the Burke brothers, sergeant.'

'Sir,' the non-com acknowledged and this was the only vocal response to confirmation of the order.

Anne Tucker groaned her intention to recover consciousness and Steele rested the rifle and placed a hand lightly over her lower face as he listened to booted feet move in the gully. The woman snapped open her eyes, closed them immediately against the harsh assault of brilliant sunlight.

'You're all right, Anne,' Steele whispered, leaning close to her.

Her lips moved under his palm and a shudder wracked her

body. Her eyes opened again and showed pain and fear. They peered into his face and for long seconds showed no hint that they recognised the features.

'We're having some of that dumb luck,' he told her softly. 'Make a sound and it could run out.'

Her eyes left his face and swung to their full extent in the sockets, peering across the rock-littered area and then back down the defile to where it curved into the gully, out of sight. The pain continued to hold a grip on her, but the look of panic abated. She brought up both her hands to gently push Steele's palm off her face. He became aware for the first time of the darkening bruise on the side of her jaw.

'You mean it?' she rasped.

He placed a finger to his own lips and nodded briefly. Then both of them listened hard to curt exchanges of words, followed by the sounds of men mounting and horses moving. Not until there was total silence did the Virginian crack his lips in a grin of cold triumph. The woman, after her momentary relief, expressed wretched dejection.

'It all happened so fast, Adam,' she muttered, shaking her head and making no attempt to lift her back up off the ground. 'Those men with masks on their faces. The wagon turnin' over. Like some crazy, mixed up nightmare. I don't remember nothin' after I started to run after you . . . '

He injected some warmth into his grin. 'Reckon you could say I bowled you over and swept you off your feet, Anne.'

Chapter Ten

The woman was able to sit up and rest her back against the rock wall. But only with pain and difficulty that caused fresh beads of sweat to ooze from the pores in her face.

'Stay here, I'll be back,' Steele told her, and set off before she could protest. She was on the point of calling after him, but when he looked grimly along the defile she clamped her lips tightly together.

He walked quickly rather than ran, aware that this was just a brief respite from the threat of capture. Dan Corder would undoubtedly come out to salvage what he could of the stock from the wrecked wagon and might be less inclined than the lieutenant to give up the chase. Or the commanding officer of Sherman might order the troop to extend the search. And certainly if the Ogallala posse reached the fort, the men forming it would keep coming.

So, eager as he was to find mounts for himself and Anne Tucker as soon as possible, Steele had to conserve his energy in the event that the loose horses evaded him. For even if the woman was able to walk, the odds against survival and freedom were long. In her present incapacitated state . . .

He saw the gelding of one of the dead Burke brothers. Drinking from a shallow pool of muddy water beside a clump of poisonous copperweed and spruce saplings. This as he rounded a curve in the new defile at the head of a north-south shallow valley.

The horse raised his head and looked toward the Virginian across forty feet. And snorted. As Steele began to close slowly on the animal, he spoke softly to it and peered further along the valley featured with brush and low mesas, lone pine trees and boulders encircled by sparse, brown grass. The team horses, still held together by their harness, were plodding slowly up the western side of the valley, more than a mile away. Blind Jake's horse was cropping at grass under a boulder on the opposite slope, no more than a quarter of a mile distant.

'It's all right feller,' Steele murmured. 'You stay just where you are. Look at you, with that saddle and bags and canteens and bedroll. You're beautiful, feller. And you need somebody to take care of you. I'll take real good care of you now your old rider can't. He did me a good favour and –'

Steele halted and reached slowly forward, caught hold of the reins and curtailed the words he had been speaking in a reassuring tone. The horse finished drinking and backed away from the pool, calm and satisfied. There was just a small adjustment necessary to the stirrups before the Virginian was able to swing up into the saddle. There he checked the canteens and found one was full, the other half full. The saddlebags held enough supplies to feed two people for at least four days providing they finished each meal feeling hungry.

He rode at an easy pace over to where the piebald gelding was grazing and saw that the blind man's horse would need a much longer period of rest before it was fully recovered from the race away from Fort Sherman. But with careful riding under a light load, he would hold up for the remainder of the afternoon.

He rode back toward the head of the valley, leading the piebald by the reins, but did not have to go too far into the defile to find Anne Tucker. The woman had covered more than three hundred feet from where he had left her: clawing and pushing at the ground with her hands and the foot of her good leg and dragging the injured limb. The effort this required and the pain it generated had drained every trace of colour from her face and caused her pants and shirt to become soaked with sweat. She managed to raise a weak smile as she rested and watched the Virginian ride up to her.

He did not respond with a similar expression as he dismounted and she got the dejected look on her face again.

'It ain't I didn't trust you to come back for me, Adam,' she said breathlessly. 'I just wanted to help.'

'You reckon you can sit a horse after that?'

She used the back of a hand to brush the sweat greasy hair off her forehead and shifted her pale-blue eyes from the black to the piebald gelding and back. 'The one with the saddle on him, I think.'

'Picked him out for you.' He dropped into a crouch beside her. 'Don't scream too loud when I move you.'

She shook her head and squeezed her eyes tight closed. 'It's a well-known fact that women can take more pain than men . . . that hurt like hell and from the look on your face you enjoyed it, you lousy sonofabitch . . . I didn't mean that – callin' you that, I mean.'

She talked to try to take her mind off the pain: paused when the first wave hit her as Steele lifted her off the ground, then again when she was astride the saddle and waiting for the intensity to lessen.

'I always look mean when I'm in trouble not of my own making,' he replied and fitted the booted foot of her good leg into a stirrup. When he moved around to the right side of the horse, she shook her head.

'No, it's better the way it is,' she explained. 'I think I can stay on this way. Long as we ride easy.'

'Fine,' he said, and picked up his Colt Hartford – there was a Winchester rifle in the saddle boot of the black horse – and swung on to the back of the piebald. 'Any time you reckon you're going to fall off, you let me know.'

She nodded, shot a glance back along the defile and then clucked the horse into motion beside that of the Virginian. After a minute or so, he ceased sneaking surreptitious looks at her. She was suffering, but holding up well: seemed to him to be pained more by emotional problems than her physical injury.

When they entered the valley the team horses were no longer in sight. They were no longer on the trail, which had angled off to the south east again from the defile where he and the woman had listened to the troopers unwittingly decide their fate. But the going looked easy enough for as far as they could see: so that they had to contend only with the harsh heat and glare of the sun and the knowledge that if they were being pursued, they would be in full view of anyone who entered the valley before they rode out of it.

'Adam?'

'Yes?'

'May I take a drink of water?'

'A mouthful is all. I'll have one, too.'

She took her ration and passed the canteen across to him. When he had taken a swig and she replaced the canteen, she said his name again.

'Yes?'

'I was an utter and complete fool back there.'

'It doesn't matter. So long as you can stay on that horse.'

'I don't mean about that. I mean about tellin' Dan Corder what happened. To Mrs Karlsen and Pa. But I did tell him it was really the Swede killed his wife.'

Steele pursed his lips. 'Another well-known fact for you. Women talk too much.'

'I didn't just tell him to pass the time of day,' she came back quickly, and resentfully.

'Reckon you didn't, Anne.'

'I figured he might help us. When he used to come by the house he always seemed like a nice, kind man. And once – not the last time he was by but the time before that – I asked him if he'd take me away with him. He said he couldn't do that. But that if I could ever get to Denver where he's got a house, he'd help me.'

She paused to invite a comment from the Virginian. But he said nothing. His expression in profile looked hardset, maybe disbelieving. The woman swallowed hard before she continued.

'I admit that when you dumped me in the back of the wagon and rode off, I was worried you wouldn't wait at Fort Sherman. That's what set me off talkin' to Mr Corder. So I guess I should have said help *me*, not *us*. And he sounded real sympathetic, so I just kept on talkin'. Who knows, maybe if he hadn't seen your horse outside the fort, he would've helped me.'

'Who knows,' Steele echoed.

'Anyway, I'm sorry, Adam. I made the trouble for you and I don't deserve what you done for me back there after the wagon tipped over. What you should've done after I shoved him off the wagon is gone in some other direction. Any way but after me.'

'But I didn't.'

'No, you didn't. And I promise I won't do anythin' else stupid.'

'Reckon one of us is enough,' Steele growled sardonically.

There was another silence. Much longer this time. Which disconcerted the woman at first, as if she felt it was directed at her. But soon she sensed Steele's tension and saw the way he continually looked back over his shoulder to check on the valley lengthening behind them. And became as content as she could be in the circumstances.

Throughout the rest of the afternoon and early evening, there was only one further exchange between them: when Steele asked for a canteen and had another mouthful of water.

They rode out of the valley as the sun touched the western horizon and a faint promise of the cool night to come was felt in the still air. Ahead of them was spread a vast expanse of plateau with a liberal scattering of steep-sided mesas. Semi-desert country, with cactus plants the highest growing vegetation amid brush and short grass. In front of the two riders, behind them and to either side, there were no signs of other human life: and no scars on the terrain to show that man had been here before.

Steele and Anne Tucker rode perhaps four miles out across the wilderness east of the Continental Divide before the sun finally slid from sight behind the distant ridges. Then, as the afterglow of its setting faded and the shadows it had cast expanded to make the darkness of full night, the Virginian pointed to a mesa a quarter of a mile ahead and a hundred feet west of their route.

'We'll bed down for the night there,' he said.

'Whatever you say, Adam,' she replied and he glanced at her for the first time in more than an hour. Saw that her tone of voice was a true pointer to how she was feeling. The battle she had been waging against the encroachment of exhaustion was almost lost: and it was sheer willpower which was keeping her in the saddle.

The light of the moon was glitteringly bright and throwing pitch-black shadows by the time they reached the foot of the mesa's eastern wall and the Virginian called a halt in the darkness under the rock face. The woman hauled on the reins to stop the gelding, but made no attempt to dismount unaided.

'I didn't know a person could feel so beat and not just fall over,' she murmured.

'Reckon it won't do any harm if you need to scream now,' he told her softly as he slid off the back of the piebald and went to her horse. He held up his arms and allowed her to make the moves that were the least painful to her.

She gritted her teeth and dug her fingers deep into his arms as he lifted her out of the saddle and lowered her to the ground. But it was a coyote, far in the distance, that howled.

'Thanks,' she managed to force out before she devoted all her concentration to containing a vocal outlet of her pain.

Steele ignored her while he unsaddled the black gelding, hobbled both horses with the reins and unfurled a dead man's bedroll. In the roll there were just two blankets, a tin mug and eating utensils and a black rain slicker.

Anne Tucker was on the verge of sleep as the Virginian draped the blankets over her but came fully awake with a startled cry as their weight covered her.

'Oh, I'm sorry,' she said.

'What for?' he answered as he sat down beside the saddle and began to unfasten one of the bags.

'Actin' like a scared rabbit. I was dozin', I guess.'

'You need sleep.' He handed her a chunk of jerked beef and a canteen. 'But you need to eat as well. Supper. Just one mouthful of water, remember.'

She accepted what was offered and raised herself up on to one elbow. Taking her cue from Steele, she made her water ration last, taking a sip to wash down each bite of tough, dried meat. When the frugal meal was over, she lay out on her back again with the blankets covering her from feet to throat and peered up at the bright pinpoints of stars spread thickly against the blackness of the sky. And said morosely:

'I guess there's no chance of gettin' back on the Swede's trail now?'

'No need. Sven Karlsen is heading for Chihuahua.'

She snapped her head around to look at the Virginian, her expression abruptly animated. 'He told somebody at Fort Sherman that?'

'He asked how far it was.'

'How far is it? Where is it, Adam?'

'Six or seven hundred miles, I reckon.'

'Wow. Sounds like it's in Mexico. You ever been to that town before? You know it?'

'Not a town. A state of Mexico.'

Her excitement diminished. 'Guess states in Mexico are big. Like in this country?'

'Big,' he confirmed. 'But they don't have so many towns in them. And a bigger-than-average man with blond hair shouldn't be too hard to find in a place filled with small, dark-haired fellers.'

'But ain't Mexico where a lot of American outlaws run to hide? Pa always said it was. Kind of country where a man could lose himself for life, if there was a rope waitin' for him north of the border.'

Steele nodded. 'That's right, Karlsen didn't ask how far it was to Mexico, though. Named Chihuahua. Reckon there has to be a good reason why he did that.'

'Hey, that's right.' She paused, then: 'You think he knows somebody down there?'

'Maybe. Or maybe somebody he met up with in prison gave him the name of a good place to run to. No point in trying to make guesses right now. You want me to take your pants off, or can you do it?'

'What?' She snapped her head to the side to stare at him again, her eyes widened by shock and fear.

Steele pursed his lips to vent a weary sigh. 'Easy,' he said. 'There have been some times when I could have made you bare assed to tan your rump. And some for another reason.' He pointed a gloved finger southwards across the plateau. 'Six or seven hundred miles, Anne. The faster I can cover them, the better. On account of I don't know how long Karlsen plans to stay in Mexico. Anything I can do to make your leg feel easier, the faster we can travel.'

'What can you do?'

'First off look at it and try not to be maddened by lust,' he muttered as he shuffled across to her on his rump.

'Oh, my,' she gasped and covered her face with her hands as he dragged the blankets off her. 'No man has ever touched me before.'

'Didn't you ever need a doctor?' he asked, and began to unbuckle her belt.

'That's different.' She shifted her hands to cover her eyes.

'We're a long way from the nearest doctor so I'll have to do. Get your rear end up off the ground.'

Her upper teeth bit down on her lower lip, but she did as he instructed, which enabled him to ease the pants off her hips and pull them down to below her knees. Her unadorned underwear reached to this level. And her cry was more of pain than fear as he gently pushed the harsh but serviceable fabric upwards to bare her slender right thigh from kneecap to hip bone. Her flesh was cool and firm, milk white except for a large and ugly purple swelling on the outside of the thigh.

'What did I do to it, Adam?' she asked tensely.

'Hit the ground hard with it. Maybe fell on a rock. There's a bad bruise on the outside. No way of telling how much damage inside. You didn't break a bone, because you wouldn't have made it this far. Maybe you cracked one. More likely tore a muscle.'

The way he was sitting with legs folded, the split seam in his pants was gaping. He reached through and pulled out the knife: then pushed it up under her shirt front. She gasped, flung her arms to the side and pushed herself up into a half-sitting posture when she felt the cold metal of the knife against her belly.

'What are you doin'?' she shrieked.

'Hold still!' he snapped. 'Or I could change from being a fake doctor to an unqualified surgeon. By a bad accident.'

She remained rigid, back canted and supporting herself on her splayed arms, as the knife sliced through her underwear. From upper to lower belly and then down each leg. Her eyes were wide but her lips were firmly compressed, trapping the breath in her body. Steele took care to ensure that her belly and upper thighs remained covered by the shirt.

'Lay back and raise your butt again, Anne,' he said.

'What are you goin' to – ?'

'Be best if we could put a cold compress on it, but we don't have the water to spare. All we can do is bind it up. Tight as you can stand it.' He showed her his boyish grin. 'I reckon the ladies of Ogallala would be shocked to know you'll be riding around with just your pants between you and the saddle, but we're fresh out of bandages.'

'Oh, this is terrible,' she moaned after releasing her pent-up breath. 'Why didn't I bounce on my head instead of there?'

'Up,' he told her.

She lay back and submitted to Steele's treatment of her injury; watched the stars while he cut her underwear into long strips and spoke just once, to let him know the most comfortable tension for the binding. She raised her rump off the ground again so that he could pull her pants back over her hips.

After he had draped the blankets back across her body, without bothering to fasten her belt buckle, he returned to his previous place. To stretch out on his back with just the rain slicker covering him, his right hand fisted around the frame of the Colt Hartford.

'Adam,' she said softly after several silent minutes had elapsed.

'Yes?'

'What kind of time was it?'

'Time?'

'When I was half naked. Did you want to beat me or do . . .'

'Go to sleep, Anne.'

'I'm sorry I didn't trust you. Later . . . When my leg is well . . . And everythin' else is right . . . Maybe then we could do what only married people are supposed to do.'

'Maybe,' he answered. 'But until morning I reckon we should do something else married folks do a lot of the time.'

'What's that?'

'Not talk to each other.'

Chapter Eleven

It took a week for Anne's leg to heal to the extent that she was able to get on and off her horse unaided and undertake her share of the few chores that were necessary when they camped. In this time they covered close to a hundred and fifty miles of the desolate terrain of southern Colorado Territory. At an easy pace which caused her the minimum of discomfort and did not take too much out of the horses.

The days were blisteringly hot and the nights were clear and cool. They replenished their water from the trickling stream that was the Arkansas River but had to pass a day and a half without food until they reached a line shack at the edge of a vast ranch. The larder in the shack was well stocked, but Steele took only enough canned and dried food to last the woman and himself five days on short rations. And left more than enough money to cover the cost of what he had taken.

They had little to say to each other during the whole week but for an hour after they rode away from the shack she maintained a constant barrage of scornful words about his decision to take such a small amount of food. Having made his point at the outset that line riders who expected the shack to be well stocked with supplies might be in greater need than he and the woman, he held his peace. And eventually she talked herself out. After which, her silence became petulantly sullen in contrast to the uncomfortably embarrassed kind which had kept her tongue tied previously.

The terrain they rode across changed little from day to day, but the most constant factor of all was the absence of other human beings. And shortly after sunrise on the eighth day, as Anne doused the fire while Steele prepared the horses, the woman said:

'I figure they've given up on us, Adam.'

Her tone was conversational, her face was devoid of sulkiness or pain and it was the first time she had used his given name since the diatribe against him after the line shack incident.

'Maybe,' he allowed as he followed her cue and peered northwards across the empty land which was now behind them.

'Or lost us. If they'd picked up our trail from Sherman surely they would've got close enough for us to have seen them by now?'

'Let's go,' he told her, holding out the reins of the black gelding.

'Mexico still?' She swung awkwardly up into the saddle before he could get into a position to help her.

'Where I'm headed,' he answered, getting astride the piebald and clucking the horse forward. 'What we agreed at the start still holds good. You can go your own way anytime you feel like it.'

'But if the Ogallala posse have given up or lost us and you got no reason to ever go to that town, why bother tryin' to find the Swede?' She sounded irritated, but suddenly she smiled and steered her horse close to the piebald. 'It's a big country outside of Ogallala. And there's a whole wide world outside of this country, ain't there? It was right what you did back at that shack. Right by the cowpunchers that work the spread. The same as you've always done right by me.'

'Grateful for the kind words,' he drawled.

She shot him a suspicious glance, as if she was half-convinced he was patronising her. But in profile his unshaven, dust-streaked face was set in its usual impassive expression.

'And I want to do right by you, Adam,' she went on. 'You're a good man who ain't been havin' too many breaks lately. But maybe I can change that. My leg feels almost good as new now. In awhile it will be as good as new. Maybe by then we'll have reached a town. With a store where I can get some pretty clothes. And a hotel with clean rooms where we can . . . '

She allowed the implied promise to hang in the warm air of

early morning. Steele did not fill the lengthening silence with words and continued to ride in his normal fashion – keeping apparently nonchalant watch on the surrounding country.

'Adam?' she encouraged eventually.

'Yes.'

'You were listenin' to what I just said?'

'Yes.'

'And you know what I was gettin' at?'

'Plain to see.'

She sighed and Steele suspected it might have been a time-consuming act while she subdued an impulse to anger. 'You make it very difficult for a girl.'

'Tell you something I don't make.'

'What's that?'

'Plans.'

'But we can now,' she said quickly. 'Now we're so far away from all the bad things that happened. We got through those bad times together pretty well. I figure we're due for some good times. And if we start them off the right way, like I was talkin' about, well I reckon everythin' will be fine for us. Especially as we're two of a kind, like you said that first day we met up.'

'You proposing to me, Anne?' he asked evenly.

'No I ain't!' she retorted. 'All I'm sayin' is that I like you. And I realise I ain't acted like it much. Best way there is for a woman like me to prove her feelin's for a man is to give herself to him. Because herself is all she has to give. And I want to. But I want it to be right. And if afterwards you figure you can forget everythin' that happened up north then I'll be ready to go on givin' myself to you.'

'Grateful to you, Anne,' he said.

'Is that all?'

'What else?'

'Go to hell!'

This was the start of another sullen silence, which lasted throughout the day as they trekked south. But during the following day her resentment abated and she began to talk freely about her past, choosing to recall the better times: and to ask casual questions about Steele's years as a drifter. She never referred to their conversation of the morning before and steered clear of any subject that might trigger thoughts of the future. And she always switched to another topic when she sensed she had awakened memories of women he had known in the past.

Thus it was that she, with the unemotional co-operation of the Virginian, brought their relationship on to an even keel – by adjusting herself to his viewpoint. Which was that in terms of their own response to each other, only the present mattered. He demanded that she keep pace with him, do her share of the camp chores and not refer to the future. Comply with these rules or leave. Beyond this, she was her own mistress. If she wanted to become his, the moment was of her own choosing.

For his part, Steele did not have to make any concessions: beyond controlling his desire for the woman. This was most necessary at night as they bedded down and in the early morning when he always awoke before her and could see her body contoured by the blankets in the first light of the new day. But the decision was her own. As far as he was concerned, the decision always belonged to the woman. Sometimes the waiting was harder to take than others.

They reached the stage trail four days after leaving the line shack. Steele guessed they had crossed the territorial boundary by then and were in New Mexico. The trail inscribed a wide curve from the north to the south west, along the base of the Rockies where they were high and then swinging into less towering peaks. Cutting through pure desert country and into scrub-covered hills.

'Thank God,' Anne said. 'A trail has to go from one place to another doesn't it?'

'Sure does,' Steele allowed as they began to ride along the clearly defined road. 'Only trouble is that out in this kind of country the places can be a long way apart.'

'You got any ideas?'

He jerked a thumb over his shoulder. 'Reckon Denver is that way.' Then nodded in the direction they were riding. 'And Sante Fe down there.'

'Sante Fe!' she repeated excitedly.

'At least four days' ride.'

'Damn!'

Steele leaned forward and used a hand to supplement the shade of his hat brim. Then he straightened up astride the piebald. 'Don't know what that place is called.'

'What place?' she demanded, snapping out of her crestfallen attitude.

'Ahead.'

They had reached the top of a slight rise and a small cluster of buildings had come into view. They straddled the trail about five miles distant: a few dark blobs on the yellow tinged desert, seeming to tremble in the shimmering heat haze – which was why Steele had done a double-take at what might well have been a mirage.

'Oh, Adam!' the woman gasped. Then veered her horse over close to his, dropped the reins, turned towards him and leaned to the side. Her arms encircled him, around the chest and shoulders, and she pressed her lips hard on his as he swung his face to look at her.

Delirious excitement had left her breathless and she had to end the kiss after a few moments to suck air into her lungs. Still clinging tightly to him, her blue eyes glittering brightly and her speech peppered with short laughs, she stammered:

'You know what we've done, Adam? We've made it! I never said so, but I didn't think we would! All that talk about the future, that was to keep me goin'! To stop me from goin' crazy! A person can get low enough to go crazy, you know? I used to come close to that shut in the house. Only way I could keep from goin' mad was daydream about somethin' better! And now all them dreams are gonna come true! I know they will!'

She spoke too loudly and too close to his ear so that many of her words were distorted. But he got the gist of what she said and for the first time since their meeting he felt admiration for Anne Tucker.

He disentangled himself from her arms and grinned as he leaned away from her. 'Let's go see where we've made it to, uh?'

She nodded vigorously. 'You bet.'

They moved their mounts forward again, towards the tiny town that had triggered her joy. To the Virginian it was just another town on another trail. The latest of many destinations he had reached, by accident or design, along the countless trails he had ridden since leaving the corpse of Jim Bishop behind him.

Bish had been his best friend. Max Tucker had been Anne's father. Which was the more heinous crime?

He shook his head, almost imperceptibly. And compressed his lips. It was a pointless exercise to draw academic distinctions. To try to see the woman in a bad light by arguing that her past wrong was greater than his own.

So, as they closed with the town, riding near enough to see individual buildings no longer blurred by the heat haze, he reflected on what the woman had said and what she had accomplished – what they both had accomplished – since they rode away from the Drover Inn.

They had covered more than three hundred gruelling miles across harsh country under a blistering sun. Living on the most frugal of rations and riding a horse or horses that for the greater part of the trip were ill-equipped and as badly provided for as Anne and himself. Trouble caused by their fellow men had been confined to the outbreaks of violence at the Drover Inn and Fort Sherman. But nature had been relentless in her constant assault against the travellers.

Only now did Steele pause to consider the extent of their deprivation and the effects it had on them – horses and riders alike.

The piebald and the black gelding were both thin and their coats lacked the lustre of good health. There was a glaze over their eyes. For the last three days their tails had hardly twitched and they seldom shook their heads to dislodge the desert flies. They were obviously drawing on their final reserves of stamina.

He glanced at the woman riding beside him. There was a smile on her face but it had only a very frail hold on her prominently boned features: poised to be shattered if the town they were approaching fell just a degree below her expectations. Her skin was no longer pale and blemish-free, for under the sweat-pasted trail dust he could see where the sun had scorched it and left ugly red blotches, some of which were peeling. Her lips were cracked and her teeth were stained. Her eyes looked sunken, this impression emphasised by the dark half-circles beneath them. The red hair hung limp and thickly matted to either side of her face. Her once slender but sensually rounded body no longer totally filled her shirt and pants, the clothes now looking to be two sizes too large for her. When she had been leaning close to him and venting her joy, he had smelt her foul breath and the rancid odour of dried sweat.

As they rode beyond the town marker, its lettering bleached out of existence by the New Mexico sun, he knew he was in as bad shape as the woman. He had lost weight and was lacking his usual physical strength and mental alertness. His breath and flesh smelled as bad as hers did. His lips were painfully cracked. Maybe the weathered skin of his face had not suffered so much from the harshness of the sun's heat but it was certainly as deeply ingrained with dirt. And the back of a gloved hand run over the flesh proved there was several days' growth of bristles covering the lower half and his throat.

So the one street town of adobe and frame-constructed buildings was not just another destination along the mostly aimless trails he rode. This one was different. For if it had not been where it was, there was a strong possibility he would not have reached it. And nature would have succeeded in what many men had attempted. The horses would have gone first, dropped by exhaustion to be finished with a bullet. Then the woman . . . Or maybe not. Perhaps her daydreams would have kept her going, long after the Virginian – lacking the ability to imagine a future filled with hope – had submitted to a brand of lethal weariness never before experienced.

'Hey, mister!' Anne called. 'What is this place?'

The short, fat, red-faced man she addressed was standing on the threshold of a store between display windows filled by hardware merchandise on one side and canned and bottled provisions on the other.

'Nowhere, ma'am,' the storekeeper answered, shifting his curious gaze back and forth between the dishevelled couple.

'It has to be somewhere!' the woman retorted shrilly, obviously on the verge of anger.

Her tone and expression disconcerted the man in the doorway. 'It is, ma'am. That's the name of the town. Nowhere. And you don't have to look far beyond the place to see why it got called that.'

Anne got the smile back across her features. 'Well, mister, to me and Adam Nowhere is the next best thing to heaven. Ain't that right, Adam?'

Steele had scanned both sides of the short street and seen that the appropriately named town was little more than an expanded stage line way station. Next to the general store there was a stage depot and beyond this a livery stable. On the other side of the broad street was a barber shop, a shack simply labelled *Souvenirs* and a hotel. All the single storey buildings in the business of supplying necessities and luxuries to the travelling public.

He curled back his sun-punished, painfully dry lips to show a smile that matched that of Anne Tucker. 'Reckon if this is second best, then the real thing has to be all they say it is.'

The storekeeper wiped sweat-tacky palms down the front of his apron, worked some saliva into his mouth and spat a big globule of it into the dusty street.

'You folks gotta be out of your minds,' he growled sourly.

Steele raked his eyes over the façades of the buildings again and broadened his grin. Then muttered: 'Maybe heaven sent.'

Chapter Twelve

First Steele saw to it that the horses were fed, watered and bedded down in the livery stable. Then he crossed the street and entered the hotel, where Anne was already eating her way through an enormous pile of steak and beans: washing down each mouthful of food with a swig of beer. He drank a cup of coffee, ate the meal and then had more coffee.

The Mexican who ran the hotel explained that the food was ready because the Wednesday stage was scheduled to roll in from the north some time in the afternoon. After drawing no response from the busily eating strangers, the Mexican shrugged and resumed his reading of a colourfully covered, dog-eared dime novel.

'You have any rooms, feller?' Steele asked after he had finished the meal. He felt full, but wearier than ever.

'*Si, señor*. Six of them, all empty. They are not much, because it is not often that people stay in Nowhere. Most times they come, they eat and the drink and they go.'

'How about a bathtub?'

'*Si.*'

'The lady will take a bath while I get a shave. Then I'll use the tub. We'll need two rooms.'

The Mexican, who was short, pot-bellied, round faced and with a bald head in middle age, licked his lips nervously. '*Señor*,' he called as the Virginian moved towards the door. 'I do not wish offence. Already I have provided food for the *señorita* and yourself. You do not look . . . I understand you have travelled far and . . . but is there money to pay for what you have had and what you ask?'

Steele had made no money since leaving Chicago and his roll was shrinking. But there was still some left. He pulled some bills from the hip pocket of his suit pants and placed a five and five ones on the table closest to the door of the spartantly furnished saloon.

'Enough, feller?'

A broad smile wreathed the Mexican's smooth face. 'More than enough, *señor*.'

'With the change, Adam!' Anne said before the Virginian could leave the place. 'If the store has dresses, may I buy one?'

'No.'

Her seductive smile, which did not fit well on her weather punished face, abruptly slipped. And she formed her lips into a sullen pout.

'But I want to look nice for you.'

'After a tub, you'll look fine,' he told her.

'Not in these clothes!' she snapped, waving her hands in front of her.

'Out of them.'

He canted the Colt Hartford to his shoulder and turned again to leave.

'But you said we need two rooms,' Anne complained, suddenly apprehensive.

'They're to sleep in,' Steele muttered, and heard a burst of laughter from the Mexican as he stepped out into the afternoon sunlight. A sound that was abruptly curtailed: perhaps by a glare from the blue eyes of the woman.

There was just one chair and one elderly barber in the parlour beyond the souvenir shack.

'Nice day,' the grey-haired, wizen faced, stoop-shouldered old-timer greeted.

'Getting better by the moment,' Steele acknowledged as he lowered himself luxuriantly into the chair. 'Shave and cut. Close shave but not too much hair off.'

'Sure thing.'

'And one answer,' Steele added as the not-very-clean cover was draped around his neck.

8

'Do my best.'

'I'm looking for a big Swedish feller with blond hair. Did he pass through town in the last few days?'

'Wednesday today, ain't it? That's right. Stage is due from the north.' He frowned in thought as he mixed up a lather. Then nodded. 'Makes you four days behind that feller. Stopped by Sunday. Just for a shave and to buy some grub from the store. Big tipper.'

'Grateful to you,' Steele said and closed his eyes as he lay his head back against the chair rest.

'Looked to be as long on the trail as you and your lady friend.'

'Ask how far it is to Chihuahua?'

'That he did.'

Steele sighed at the pleasant feel of cool lather on his face. And for the duration of the shave and the haircut that followed had to make an effort to stay awake.

Things were looking good and he experienced a warm, restful glow of pleasure and contentment. The not-very-bright Sven Karlsen was leaving an easy trail to follow and only had a four-day lead. One extra day would not make too much difference.

If the Ogallala posse were still in pursuit, the men in it would not take the time to rest up. But since the Drover Inn there had always been doubt about the very existence of such a posse. In the back of his mind, he hoped the new sheriff was leading a group of deputies south. For if they were close by when he found the Swede, it would be better if the Ogallala men learned the truth directly rather than via some local lawman down on the border.

This was a purely selfish attitude, of course, which took no account of Anne Tucker's position. But even before he lowered himself into the comfort of the chair in the barber shop, he had already discounted the woman as no more than another pleasure to be enjoyed in Nowhere, New Mexico Territory. Before, rested up, he started out again for somewhere in Chihuahua, Mexico.

He paid the barber and from the old-timer's grin and bright 'Good luck, stranger', guessed his tip was bigger than the one Karlsen had left.

Outside, as some of the heat of the afternoon began to dissipate, an emaciated young Apache Indian said from within the souvenir shack: 'Guess you don't wanna buy any beads or jewellery or stuff like that for the lady, mister?'

'I've done all I need to for her, feller,' Steele replied as he continued on to the hotel.

'The *señorita* is finished with the tub, *señor*,' the Mexican said, glancing up from his book. 'It is in the back room, through there.'

He nodded toward an open doorway at the end of the bar counter.

'I fear she is not happy,' the hotel man went on. 'She used much bad language and spilled much water.'

'She's a lady who likes to have her own way.'

A knowing nod before the Mexican returned to his reading, and muttered: 'Once I have wife like that.'

Anne's dirty water had been tipped away. Steele refilled the tub from the two large pots on the range and for long minutes enjoyed a simple pleasure that surpassed the brand he had relished in the barber shop chair. As then, his weariness increased. But so did the urgency of his need for the woman. He tried to subdue this, but his mind refused to blot out remembered images. Of her covered breasts nudging his back as they rode double on the stallion. Of the lust he had joked about but felt strongly when he half-undressed her to check on her injured leg. Of his coupling with Lydia Karlsen which had pushed him out on to yet another tightrope of life and death.

'The door there gives on to the rooms of the hotel, *señor*,' the Mexican announced when Steele emerged, clean body dressed in travel stained clothes. 'I gave the *señorita* the keys for rooms four and five.'

'You give her my change, too?' the Virginian asked as he pulled open a door in the corner, along from that which gave on to the kitchen.

'*Si*. Five dollar and fifty cents. Perhaps I should tell you she went to the store. She bought something. Small. Not a dress.'

'Grateful to you.'

Beyond the door was a short, dark hallway, the window at the far end too filthy to admit much of the day's fading sunlight.

But it was sufficient for Steele to see the numerals painted crudely on the three doors to either side.

'Is that you, Adam?' Anne called nervously from behind the door of room four as Steele's footfalls sounded on the boarded floor.

'Right first time.'

'I'm very tired.'

'That's for married people,' he answered, noting that the key was in the outside of the lock of door five.

'Please, Adam,' she said with a tremor in her voice. Almost as if she was on the verge of tears. 'I think we should get some sleep first.'

He reached out a gloveless hand. The knob turned but the door would not open. He heard the woman's sharp intake of breath. Then:

'It's locked. And if you try to break in the room, I'll –'

Steele had already raised a foot off the floor. And her voice was abruptly curtailed as he leaned back, kicked his leg forward and hit the door with a boot heel.

The door swung open, the woman screamed, the door hit the wall and Steele thrust the Colt Hartford into the gap.

'Oh God!' she gasped. And threw aside the tiny gun which had been fisted in her right hand.

She was sitting up in the narrow bed. Still dressed – above the waist at least. But, just as if she had been naked, she grabbed at the blankets and jerked them up to her throat. Terror was etched deep into the flesh of her face which was now clean and shiny: childlike between the lank strands of her damp red hair.

Anne had mistaken the reason for the levelled rifle, which now served the purpose Steele intended – kept the door from banging back into its frame after bouncing off the inner wall of the room.

Only by a furrowing of his brow and a narrowing of his eyelids did the Virginian reveal his displeasure at her actions: as he shifted his gaze from her face to the discarded derringer and back. This as he stepped over the threshold, canted the rifle to his shoulder and closed the door at his back.

'I frighten you that much, Anne?' he asked softly and looked around the room.

The Mexican had warned him not to expect too much. It was about twelve by twelve with whitewashed adobe walls, a timber ceiling with a kerosone lamp hanging from its centre and a board floor. A ceramic crucifix was nailed to the wall above the bed. There was a bureau against a wall with a tin basin and pitcher on it. A stool was placed under the only window which offered, through a moth-eaten piece of net curtain, a view of evening falling over the trail-bisected country to the north of Nowhere.

Far off among the long shadows cast by the sinking sun something was moving, leaving a dust cloud in its wake. The southbound stage, he guessed, running late.

'I wouldn't have shot you, Adam,' Anne forced out from her constricted throat. 'I bought the gun just to ... to protect myself.'

'From who?'

Her eyes were trapped by his level gaze, but she managed to escape: bent her head to look down at her fingers clawed over the tops of the blankets. She was looking and sounding more childlike by the moment.

'I don't want to, Adam.'

'Because I said no to a dress?'

He went to the stool, leaned the rifle against it and then took off his hat and the scarf with the weighted corners.

'What?'

'A town with a store where you could buy a dress and we could get cleaned up.'

He took off his vest and began to unbutton the lace-trimmed shirt.

'But I told you. I said all that talk was just to keep up my spirits. The same kind of thing I used to think about when the times were real bad with Pa.'

'You know something, Anne?' he drawled as he lay his shirt atop the other clothes on the stool.

'What?' She continued to half-sit, half-lay in the bed, head bowed. Obviously aware of what he was doing: perhaps even watching him fearfully out of the corner of her eye, peering between the fall of damp hair.

'You're not a little girl anymore.'

'I know that!'

'Another thing you know is that you're alone in the world now. That big wide world you talked about.'

'So?' she posed as he moved to the bed, clad only in pants and longjohns.

'You're a bright young lady. You learn fast. You've been through hell, done some things right and some wrong. When they were wrong, you learned by your mistakes. Only thing you haven't learned is that nothing is for nothing. And it could just be better for you that I teach you the lesson.'

He reached down, grasped a corner of the blankets and wrenched them off her. She tried to scream, but the sound remained trapped in her throat for part of a second: then emerged as a strangled choke.

Silence then, except for the small noises Steele caused as he unfastened her clothes and took them off her. It was as if she was unconscious again, her eyes closed and her limbs limp: so that she neither struggled against him nor moved a muscle to help him as he raised her back to pull the shirt off her shoulders and her rump to ease the pants away from her.

For a time his own arousal was in danger of diminishing as he experienced a rising anger. Directed in part at the woman for her total lack of response and inwardly because of a nagging sense of shame that threatened his resolve. But then, when she was naked his desire – he refused to acknowledge it as lust – to possess her was as strong as ever. For there was nothing child-like about her nude body stretched out on the mattress: its angles and curves, indentations and high points, hirsute areas and expanses of smooth skin clear to see in the twilight creeping through the window.

Her face, despite the sun burn, looked very pale amid the dark hair spread on the pillow to either side. Fear had left it now and her expression was a strange one of sullen repose. She was as submissive as from the beginning when, after he had taken off his pants and underwear, he eased her thighs apart. But then, as she felt the bed sink under his weight, she clenched her fists at her sides and parted her lips to hiss between clenched teeth:

'If you hurt me, I'll kill you. Some time, somehow, I'll find you and I'll kill you, Adam.'

'Just pay attention to the lesson, Anne,' he replied softly. 'In the big wide world there's no pleasure without pain. Nothing is for nothing. Through with words for awhile.'

He needed no preliminaries and it was obvious she would gain nothing from them. Her flesh was cold, so there was not even the beads of sweat to make the entry easy.

She caught and held her breath as he guided himself against the obstacle. Then released the air with a shriek as he plunged down and through and into her. Liquid warmth surrounded him. And the tackiness of her sweat was transferred to his flesh.

'Kill you, you bastard!' she forced out as the pain held at a high peak and she snapped open her eyes to stare hatefully up at his face, no more than six inches above her own. Her body was rigid.

'No words for awhile,' he murmured, holding still inside her and having to struggle against the urge for immediate release.

He could hear the stage now. The thud of hooves and creaking of wheels and springs: the cadence of the sounds falling as the driver slowed his team for the stopover in Nowhere.

Under him, Anne closed her eyes and her teeth parted between her already open lips. The muscles of her body relaxed. Then tensed again. Her thighs widened and she raised her arms. He felt her fingernails like talons on his back.

He began to move.

She groaned. Then gasped. Pushed her belly up hard against his. Moved her torso so that the suddenly erect nipples of her small breasts inscribed sensual patterns among the hairs on his chest.

She began to breathe in time with his movements. Then to match her actions to his. Her legs parted to their full extent and her feet dropped to the floor at either side of the bed. This gave her extra purchase to force herself up against him. Her need for release became urgent and she swung her head from side to side on the pillow.

'I – ' she began. But the ecstacy of climax struck her dumb. And exhaustion drained the strength from her body.

Steele completed the act a beat later and Anne gasped and

clung to him during the moments of his jerking release. They tremored and held tight to one another as their mingled sweat became suddenly cold.

'He deserved it,' she whispered, her lips moving against his ear as, out on the street, the stage came to a halt and men exchanged shouts of greeting and traded answers for questions.

'Reckon I did.'

'Yes. I'm sorry. Thank you, Adam. But I mean my father.' Her tone became embittered. 'I'm past twenty-five. A long time since I was a child. And he kept me from this.'

Steele eased out of her and up from her. She was reluctant to let him go, but did not have the strength to retain her hold.

'There's lots of time left, Anne,' he told her, as he draped the blankets back over her. 'And a world full of men. Just take care over the ones you choose. Or just one would be best.'

He started to dress. It was almost full night now, but in the moonlight he could see she was watching him.

'You don't want to be that one?' she asked, her voice melancholic.

'In lots of things, the first isn't always the best.'

She remained quiet until he was almost dressed: pants and boots, his shirt and vest on but not buttoned, hat on and scarf draped around his neck – the knife strapped to his leg.

Then: 'And you're goin' to Mexico to find Sven Karlsen so everyone'll know you didn't kill Lydia.'

'Sure,' he answered, canting the Colt Hartford to his shoulder.

'And that'd be a waste of time. If you was ridin' for ever more with someone lots of people saw kill a person?'

He stooped to pick up the small derringer. A two-shot Remington like one he owned a long time ago.

'We never get everything we want in the world, Anne,' he told her. 'It's seldom that simple.'

She rolled her head on the pillow and stared up at the ceiling. 'Do one more thing for me. Please?'

'What's that?'

'The gun cost three dollars. There's a real pretty dress over at the store. It's four dollars. I figure the man will take the gun back and let me have the dress if I pay the extra.'

Steele tossed the gun on to the bed. 'Keep the dollar fifty you'll be left with, Anne,' he said, and went out of the room.

Although the lock was broken, the door stayed closed. He went into room five which was furnished in precisely the same way as the one he had just left. He took off only his boots and hat before he stretched out on top of the bed, the Colt Hartford beside him.

The peace of mind and pleasant physical weariness he had felt in the barber chair and in the bath tub were nothing to what he experienced now. As a sexual partner, the novice Anne Tucker did not compare with any woman he had ever taken. But he had expected no more: for the fulfilment of desire had been of secondary importance. She had owed him and the debt was paid. He had had the courage to extract the debt: and had demanded it in such a way that he felt neither shame nor guilt.

The money for the dress? If ever he had cause to regret spoiling a virgin against her will he would be able to combat such unbidden thoughts with the knowledge that Anne Tucker had suggested the transaction: that today she was a four dollar whore and he was a big tipper.

'Hey, Mr Sanders! It's Annie Tucker!'

Steele was only moments way from much needed sleep when he heard the shouted words. And recognised they were yelled by the youngster named Quint. He tightened his grip around the Colt Hartford and folded his back up off the bed. How long since he left her? Long enough for her to dress and step out on to the street with the gun and the rest of the money for the dress? Long enough for her to have made the purchase? He didn't know. It didn't matter.

He swung his legs to the floor and pulled on boots without hose. Then put on his hat. There was nothing else. The rest of his stuff had been abandoned with the black stallion at Fort Sherman.

Why did it matter Quint Ulane and Jay Sanders and maybe some more men from Ogallala had caught up with Anne? Certainly because through her they could get to him. Did his concern go beyond this to include the woman for her sake?

'Shit!' Steele rasped in angry response to the futile line of thought as he wrenched open the door.

He vented the curse as Anne shrieked: 'You bastards, you spoiled it!'

Her words were in turn shrilled over Jim Adler's bellowed plea: 'See sense, Miss Tucker!'

The pot-bellied Mexican and the elderly barber had been playing cards for matchsticks. They pulled up short, halfway to the front of the saloon, as the Virginian emerged heavy footed from the back of the place. The threat of violence which had disturbed the quiet night etched expressions of apprehension into their faces.

'*Señor*, Nowhere is not much, but always it has had peace.'

'I've never been here before,' Steele growled as he veered around them. 'Attend to your own business and I reckon I won't ever come here again.'

He halted beside the open doorway, careful not to silhouette himself against the light.

'Careful we don't have to bury you here, son,' the shrivelled-up barber warned grimly.

Steele ignored the comment and surveyed the street which was lit and shadowed by the glittering moon and the softer wedges of yellow that splashed from building windows.

There were only people on the broad area between the facing buildings, for the stage had been turned into the space between the depot and the livery for the team to be changed.

There had been time for Anne to buy and put on the dress. A white one with a high neck, puff sleeves, tight bodice and full skirt. Time, also, for her to see that the men from Ogallala were in the stage depot before they spotted her.

Perhaps there had been no opportunity for her to recross the street to the hotel. Maybe she suspected Sanders and the others would surely find out about the two strangers in town. So she had not bided her time in the store until the stage left.

Instead, she had gone across the back lots of the buildings. Into the livery and out of it, in possession of the Winchester rifle which had belonged to one of the long dead Burke brothers. And now she stood with it, cocked and levelled, in the centre of the street out front of the livery.

Some twenty feet in front of her was Jim Adler who had probably gotten over his head cold now. The moustached Jay

Sanders and the wiry, pale faced Quint Ulane were standing on the threshold of the stage line depot.

Adler, who had his back to Steele, was wearing a long coat, tightly buttoned and showing no bulge of a gun on either hip. The hands hanging at his sides were empty.

Sanders and Ulane were sideways on to the Virginian. Both wore jackets, unbuttoned and pulled back on the right where their hands draped the butts of holstered revolvers.

Steele was unable to see if any of the men wore stars. Or if there were any other men in the stage depot who might have more than a mere passing interest in what was happening.

He sensed watching eyes, glanced across at the doorway of the store and saw the aproned owner withdraw hurriedly back across the threshold. The man slammed the door closed and the sudden sound caused Sanders and Ulane to snap their heads around.

Steele made an impulsive decision and stepped out on to the street. Like the woman, he levelled his cocked rifle from the hip, but aimed it into the space between Adler and Sanders and Ulane.

'He's still with her, Jim!' Sanders snarled to the man who did not turn at the sound of the slammed door.

'Look Miss Tucker,' Adler said. 'Can you hear what I'm sayin', Steele?'

'I hear!'

'Folks in Ogallala know how it was between you and your father. Reason we couldn't raise a legal posse to come after you. But Max Tucker was a good lawman. We have to keep runnin' the town the way he did if we want it to stay decent. Come back with us, Miss Tucker. You'll stand fair trial for second degree murder and I guarantee you won't – '

'What about Adam?' the woman cut in.

'He'll get a fair trial, same as you.'

'And hang!' Jay Sanders snarled, the tic jerking the flesh under his right eye. As he stared hatefully along and across the street at the Virginian.

'Don't, Anne!' Steele roared.

But his plea was lost under the crack of the Winchester. As

the woman swung it to the right and squeezed the trigger while the muzzle was still tracking.

Her luck with a bow and arrow did not hold for the rifle. The bullet was blasted out of the barrel a part of a second too soon. And it was the young Quint Ulane who felt its impact: taking it low down in his belly. He screamed in shock rather than pain and was sent staggering back into the stage line depot.

The abruptly afraid Jay Sanders drew his revolver while Ulane was still on his feet. And he and Steele squeezed their triggers to fire shots which covered the thud of the youngster's body hitting the floor.

Steele knew he was a split-second too late. For it was necessary to throw the stock of the rifle up to his shoulder and align the sights on the narrow, sideways on target of Sanders. As he did this, he got a blurred impression of the man drawing and aiming the revolver: and of the woman in the new white dress reeling backwards under the recoil of the Winchester.

Then he saw the hole appear in Sander's right temple – and blood spurt from the wound. The man's mouth gaped, but no sound emerged. He fell hard against the doorframe, stayed there for a moment and slid down into an untidy, unmoving heap.

Anne Tucker became inert a moment later. Sprawled out on to her back, the rifle no longer in her hands. An ugly dark stain expanded across the pure whiteness of the dress fabric under her left breast.

Adler was as unmoving on his feet as the two corpses on the ground: his back still to the Virginian.

'I'm not armed, mister!' he called huskily to break a tense silence of several seconds which followed the killings.

Steele had not re-cocked the rifle. As he canted it to the shoulder, he glanced into the hotel entrance.

'Grateful if you'd bring me a blanket,' he said.

'*Si señor*,' the Mexican gasped, and hurried to get what was needed.

'You hear me, Steele?' Adler shouted.

'Relax, feller.'

The storekeeper eased open the door from his premises and came nervously outside. The man who ran the stage-line depot and the liveryman showed themselves at the rear of the Concord. Steele started along the street, trailed by the barber and then the Mexican carrying a blanket. The Apache remained in his shack, but the Virginian sensed his watching eyes behind the darkened window.

Adler glanced into the depot as Steele came level with him. 'The damn fool Ulane looks to be dead,' he muttered.

'Here, *señor*.'

Steele took the blanket and acknowledged it with a nod.

'What I said about keepin' our town decent and law abidin' is the reason I'm here, mister,' Adler assured, a great sadness replacing the fear and shock on his face.

'Fine ambition,' Steele replied as he approached the corpse of Anne Tucker.

'Was true about no one wantin' to come after her, too. Except that crazy Quint Ulane who only wanted some excitement outta Ogallala.'

'Like Anne,' Steele muttered, just loud enough for his own ears.

'But Jay, he was different,' the sole survivor from the Nebraska town left in the place called Nowhere said. 'Can only figure that with him it was guilt. It was Jay who gave Lydia Karlsen money. Every time he went out to the house to see her while the Swede was in prison. Had to be. Only way to figure it. Way he was so hell bent on catchin' up with you and takin' you back. Or killin' you.'

'Sure,' Steele allowed as he set aside his rifle and began to wrap the blanket around the dead body of Anne Tucker. She had been limp and unresponsive in his arms before. Never more so than now.

'Lousy thing for a man to do,' Adler went on. 'Take advantage of a man bein' in prison to use his wife. Guess that has to be the way he was thinkin'. Hoped to salve his conscience by hangin' the killin' on you so Karlsen could go free. Never know for sure now.'

'Karlsen won't go free,' Steele said as he continued to sit on his haunches beside the covered corpse of the woman. 'One of the things you can be sure of.'

'Your decision, mister,' Adler said dully. 'Puts you on the

side of law and order. So what happened here tonight, I guess it means you were doin' what you could to see that the truth came out. So justice could be done. Way I'll tell it to the folks back in Ogallala.'

'Fine,' the Virginian said, fisted a hand around the frame of the Colt Hartford and rose to his feet. Took one final look at the blanket swathed form and turned to head back for his room at the hotel. 'Then for now, that . . .

. . . WRAPS IT UP.'*

* Until Steele resumes his search for Sven Karlsen. And in the process meets a man called Edge.

THE END

THE GEORGE G. GILMAN
APPRECIATION SOCIETY